Life Written with God's Pen

A MOTHER'S ODYSSEY TO FREEDOM

Stella L. Reilly

Authentic Endeavors Publishing
Clarks Summit, PA

Authentic Endeavors Publishing
P.O. Box 704
Clarks Summit, PA 18411
www.authenticendeavorspublishing.com

Cover and Interior Design: Ambicionz
www.ambicionz.com

Life Written with God's Pen / Stella L. Reilly. —1st ed.
ISBN 978-0-9982105-1-3

Dedication

I dedicate this book to my parents, who were born to love and give their all to their children. Their existence and presence in my life was my reason for joy. The most precious gift they gave me was their pure and unconditional love; the kind of love that becomes a shield to save one from harm and the pains of life. Their love has given me strength and tenacity throughout my life.

I love you both beyond the definition of the word "love." Though you are gone, you are always with me, in my heart and soul, in every single day, in every step I take, until the day we will be together again.

I also dedicate this book to women; girls, sisters, mothers, and wives all over the world, with great hope that my story will give you the hope when life seems hopeless, faith when you are frightened and courage to fight without giving up, even when you are feeling tired and betrayed. Be true to yourself and I promise, you will embrace the light of life in the end.

One

"For years I've been looking for a girl with your looks," he said with a smile. "I have a movie script, but couldn't find the actress I had envisioned until I spotted your innocent face, classically beautiful without makeup. Do you know that you look like Jennifer Jones?

I shook my head, saying, "No, I don't know her." He then looked straight into my eyes and with a serious tone asked, "Are you interested in acting in movies?"

I had been waiting for this moment my whole life. I was so excited that despite not knowing who Jennifer Jones was, I immediately responded loudly, "Yes, yes, I'd love to!"

Later, the reality of what I had said hit me. I was only fifteen, too young to make such a decision. I knew I had to get my parents' permission. It was not going to be easy, but I wanted to be a movie star.

I was born in Tehran, Iran, into a loving Christian, Armenian family. My childhood was comfortable and very happy, a life filled with love, safety, and adventure. Summer was the most exciting season of all. The schools closed for the months of June, July, and August.

My father would take the family for summer vacation as our reward for doing well in school. We would travel all over Iran, one summer to the north, the next summer to south, then to the eastern and western regions.

These trips became unforgettable, thanks to my father. Each was like a classroom, giving us the chance to learn about different ways of life and all kinds of people, who would speak different dialects. We saw old cities and ancient monuments and made friends wherever we went.

Back at home and in school, there were no issues. Teachers would tell my mother not to bother with quarterly parent-teacher meetings: I was at the top of my class and well behaved. Only once had I been scolded, for calling a fourth-grade classmate a "fatty." My favorite teacher scolded, "This is your first and last time to address a classmate as fat. Shame on you, Linda."

I learned a good lesson and had no further problems at school. During those years, my priorities were school, my friends, fashionable clothing and winning basketball and volleyball games. Later on, boys were added to my list of favorite things.

Passion for life ran through my blood, and that is how I lived. My hobbies and talents kept me busy: basketball, volleyball, fencing, gymnastics, and singing in our high school choir. In particular, when singing or listening to music, I would be transported by the melody. The sweet journey would nourish my soul. I loved singing, acting, playing musical instruments, writing and dancing. I wanted to do it all.

There were six of us, Mom and Dad, three girls and a boy. The first born was my sister, Narine. When she was three, I was born, and three years later, my brother Edwin was born. When I was thirteen, my second sister, Anais was born.

Compared to my siblings, I was a bold child. My mother used to call me "walking trouble." I would always find a way to do whatever I wanted to do.

Like most women of her generation, my mom was a devoted wife and mother, always putting us before everything. However, she was a disciplinarian, too. At times, when mad at me, she would claim to wish she had had five boys instead of me. Was I giving her more trouble than would five boys?

"How many times do I have to tell you to clean your room? How often must I remind you not to hang around with kids of whom I don't approve? You cannot do whatever you want to do. Now come and apologize, come here and say that you are sorry and promise it won't happen again."

These were some of her constant admonitions. I hardly would apologize, thinking that I had not done anything wrong. I merely was curious, as if on a discovery mission.

When my mom would not get the apology or realized her words didn't work, she would try other ways to make me understand. She would chase me, but I was a fast runner. In frustration, she would throw her slipper in my direction, but it would always miss its target and occasionally, even shatter a window.

೭⦆❀⦅೮

"Are you interested in acting in movies?" I could not sleep for weeks. I wanted to stay awake throughout the quietness of the night to hear the director's words. I wanted to keep his voice in my head forever.

"Are you interested in acting in movies?"

I had dreamed of becoming an actress for a long time, constantly picturing myself as a famous movie star. It was my singing in a choir that had opened the door to acting, bringing me to the offer of a lifetime, something that filled my now sleepless nights.

Often our choir would sing backup at radio or TV stations or recording studios. It was during one of those recording sessions at a movie studio, singing a song for an upcoming movie, that I recognized a very famous face, an Armenian man, considered the Alfred Hitchcock of Iranian movie directors.

Everyone in our choir had already noticed and recognized him. It was very exciting to have him, in person, just a few steps away. During a break, we gathered to talk about him and schemed about how we could approach him to ask for his autograph.

Suddenly, one of the choir members signaled to the rest of us that he was approaching. He came closer, looking straight at me with an intense glare. I panicked, thinking maybe my voice was out of tune, and he was going to embarrass me in front of everyone. My hands and knees were shaking. I must have looked like a deer in headlights.

He came very close to me while touching his mustache and smiling. When he started to talk, I was about to faint. He told me I looked like Jennifer Jones, and he had been searching for a beautiful, innocent face to play the leading female role.

"Are you interested in acting in the movies?" He added, "Of course it is not going to start soon, this is a future project."

Without any hesitation or thought, I answered, "Yes, I would love that so much, thank you." He smiled again, kindly touched my chin and left.

The girls surrounded me with excitement. Everybody had something to say. "Did you hear what he said, that's huge." "How fantastic, my friend will be a movie actress." "Do you think you can act?"

I could not hear them. Their words were fading into the air. My head was spinning. I lost my voice in an out-of-body experience. When I finally pulled myself together, the first thing that came to mind was how I could share this with my parents.

Although my father appreciated the arts, he likely would not feel the same about having a daughter who was an actress. Not many families, especially not a traditional Armenian family such as ours, would agree to that.

Not many Iranian families appreciated the performing arts, as my family did. It seemed the stage was considered a cursed place filled with indignity. Families preferred their daughters to finish their education, find a decent man, get married and have babies, living within the boundaries of an ordinary, dictated, traditional way of life.

I knew what my parents' response would be. However, I had to ask them, had to try to convince them. Acting would fulfill my dream.

Two

The opportunity to approach my parents came one evening after dinner. When I had finished my homework, I joined the rest of the family, who were watching TV in the living room.

During a commercial break, my dad lit a cigarette, and my mother's voice filled the room.

"How many times do I have to tell you not to smoke?" Mom started to nag. "Why are you teaching your children to pick up the bad habit of smoking?" Then she left the room, pretending the smoke caused her to cough.

Not really listening to my mom's words, I signaled to Narine and Edwin that I was going to tell Mom and Dad about the director's offer. They were already in on the secret.

Narine nervously rose from her seat to leave the room. As the older sibling with the role of mentor, Narine did not want to be present to face the accusation of failing her responsibility.

Edwin, my dear brother, grinning mischievously, kept Narine in the room by giving her an ashtray and asking her to pass it to Dad. Meanwhile, Mom returned with a tray of tea for my father, asking Narine to move the little table closer to Dad's seat. Poor Narine was stuck. She had to stay.

I was scared, and nervous, too, not of my parents but about their answer. I knew the discussion would not last long because the movie would start in a few minutes, which might be to my advantage. I was hoping that just to keep me quiet during the movie, they would just say, "Yes."

I swallowed nervously and said "Dad, I'm sure you know Zaven Malaian, the famous Armenian movie director. I met him the other day at the music studio. He even spoke to me; can you believe that Zaven Malaian talked to me? You should have seen the girls' surprised and jealous faces.

"Anyway, he offered me the part of the female lead role in his next movie. It's based on an old Armenian folk story, The Lalvar's Prey. You know that story; I have seen the book in your library. So, what do you think, Dad? Aren't you impressed?"

Then nervously I turned to my mom and asked her "Mom isn't this great news? Can you picture me as a movie actor?"

I was talking so fast and excitedly that I had to stop to catch my breath. Before I could say another word, the answer sprang in unison from their lips, "No!"

Dad smiled, and in a kind tone, said, "Your singing career is already taking much of your time. Do not forget about your school and education. We prefer you sing than play a part in a movie, even though it is a very famous Armenian story. Now everybody, let's watch part two and see the nasty surprises it holds."

That was it. I had missed my opportunity. I had foolishly hoped they would say yes, but I knew if I insisted and brought the subject up again, they might become furious. We might start arguing, and I did not want that, not now, especially with my father.

I did not want to create a situation where Dad might criticize me. His respect and trust were something very precious to me, I did not want to jeopardize that.

I had to wait. I was only fourteen, not old enough to make life-changing decisions. I had to wait until I was eighteen. That seemed a thousand years away. My dream was not going to happen just yet, and life would have other surprises in store for me.

Meanwhile, at school, I talked with two of my close friends about starting a band that I wanted to name "Happy Girls." We discussed who would do what. One of the girls, Diana, had to start taking lessons so she could be the drummer. My other friend, Rita, was to take bass guitar lessons, and I had to learn to play lead guitar and would be the singer. I thought the idea was exciting. We would be the first girl band in the country.

To my huge disappointment, my friends could not convince their parents to allow them to be in a band and would not pay a penny for lessons. A girl group was unheard of in Iran.

As a punishment for my crazy idea and suggesting it to my friends, their parents told them not to socialize with me other than school projects. I found it very unfair. I did not suggest anything wrong or indecent, just to start a band.

෴

In 1967, our choir was one of few selected by the Ministry of Culture and Art to perform at the crowning ceremony of the Shah of Iran. We all were so excited and proud. This was going to be my very first income from singing.

After the crowning ceremony, the Shah would walk outside the ceremonial building where all the dignitaries and royalty from different countries were waiting to see the crowned king and queen.

We were to sing a song specially composed for the occasion while Shah and Shahbanoo, the king and queen, would greet guests. Everyone was waiting to see them wearing their crowns for the very first time.

The girls in the choir wore full-length dresses of white silk with white shoes, all custom made for the occasion by a famous designer. We were each given a beautifully made tiara to complement our dresses. The boys wore black suits with white shirts, black shoes, and ties. We all looked royally elegant.

Because of the tight security, we had to be ready by five o'clock in the morning on the day of the ceremony. For all the girls in our choir "ready by five in the morning" meant that we had to go to the hair salon the day before and sleep through the night without destroying the new hairstyles. I had to sleep face down on my pillow, the only position that wouldn't ruin my hair, but my excitement kept me awake all night, anyway.

Like millions of others, my family would be watching the ceremony on TV. Early in the morning, before leaving, I noticed the proud look on my dad's face, while my mother kept kissing me a hundred times. It felt good to see them so happy and proud of me.

I was relieved that the long, sleepless night was finally over. We all met at the Rudaki Opera Hall and boarded the waiting bus, which took us to Golestan Palace where the crowning was to take place.

Golestan Palace is one of the oldest palaces in Tehran and has world heritage status. Forty-one years before, Reza Shah Pahlavi (King Reza Pahlavi) the father of Mohammad Reza Shah Pahlavi (King Mohammad Reza Pahlavi) was also crowned here.

Even though we were traveling very early in the morning, we saw the streets slowly growing crowded as people began to gather to watch the Royal Carriage of the Shah and Shahbanoo being pulled by eight horses. The little Prince Reza would be in another carriage.

This day was also the Shah's birthday. Though the early morning air was chilly, the autumn sun was generously shining and warming the city.

On the bus, we all sat quietly; some because of excitement, others because they were still sleepy. The drive lasted close to half an hour. Upon our arrival, we were escorted by military guards and secret service agents through the gates. Our choir was going to perform outside the main building. I felt disappointed. I wanted to be inside the building where the crowning would take place, witnessing every moment of this historic event.

We were told by our conductor to be alert to his signal, and an hour later we received it. During our performance, we saw the king and the queen, followed by Prince Reza, who at that time, was seven years old. They walked gracefully, smiling happily at their guests, wearing large crowns decorated with precious stones.

While singing, I thought to myself, "How could their heads carry such heavy crowns?" The young prince impressed me. I was amazed by his ability to handle the situation so masterfully. He was holding himself like a grown man.

The Shah was in his military uniform. His many medals were shining brightly as they were struck by the bright rays of the sun, giving him a regal aura, and Shahbanoo, our new crowned Queen, wore a long white dress with a long dark green cloak, marvelously decorated with precious stones.

The Shah wanted his crowning to be a national event rather than international; that was why the leaders of foreign countries were not invited to the ceremony, only their ambassadors were present. There was one exception. His Highness Prince Karim Aga Khan IV, the 49th Imam of the Ismaili Muslims, and his wife, Begum Salimah, were the only foreign royal guests, likely because of their close friendship with the Shah.

For the first time in Iranian history, an Iranian Queen was crowned. This was an extraordinarily huge step towards women's equality in my country.

Foreign news anchors and photographers were everywhere. I enjoyed the clicking of the cameras, and I so loved to be photographed. I wished I knew who the photographers were; I would have asked for a copy of a picture for myself.

Performing at the crowning event was such an honor and privilege for our choir; we were also paid a good bit of money for our performance. I spent my portion of the money on a beautiful antique china cabinet for my mother. As for my father, he was happy to brag for almost a year afterward about his daughter singing at the royal coronation ceremony.

At seventeen, I managed to talk my parents into allowing me to do some modeling and play in short commercial clips and photo shoots. These ads were common, performed by many young girls and boys.

I had to reason with my parents and promise them that I was not going to appear in any commercial clip that would be unacceptable to them. I was already familiar with the performing arts, and I had found my passion. I also sang at the Rudaki Opera Hall, at recording studios, and at radio and TV stations for different musical shows.

At that time of my life, these were the things I loved to do. The money was good, and I eventually made enough to be financially independent. At my young age, this newly won freedom was very precious to me.

At nineteen, luck knocked on my door again. Approached to act in a movie as the leading female, I was now legally old enough to make my own decisions, but I wanted my family's approval, which would still be tough to get. But I had made up my mind, whether they approved or not, I was going to accept the offer. This was my dream. No one would stop me this time.

This fateful decision changed my whole life and began the dramatic unfolding of my destiny.

Three

A few days after accepting the offer to play the female lead in the movie, I went to the production company to be introduced to the director, the director of photography, the screenwriter, and many others. My heart was beating so fast I thought it would jump out of my chest.

I was fascinated by the presence of so many stars. To be in the same room with them was breathtaking. I had seen so many of them in movies or their pictures on the cover of the magazines, but now I was among them, as one of them.

I was introduced to Bijan Valayati, a very famous and handsome Iranian actor, as my co-star. He greeted me warmly, holding my hand in his, and said, "Hi, my name is Bijan. Glad to meet you, Linda."

He noticed my surprise but continued, "Don't be surprised, I already know your name, and have recently seen your pictures. The camera loves your face. You are very photogenic."

"I also know your name," I said, "I have seen your picture on the cover of magazines. I am very pleased to meet you. By the way, should I take your words as a compliment or do my photographs look prettier than I actually am?"

He smiled, looked at our producer and said, "I like her sense of humor and sharpness."

During the day, while going through different aspects of my contract and the storyline of the movie, the producer advised me to change my Armenian surname.

When I asked the reason, I was told that in some Iranian cities, some Muslims might resist going to my movies because of my Christian religion. By changing my last name, it would be difficult for people to know my religion so it wouldn't impact my career or ticket sales.

It sounded crazy and a bit unrealistic, but I was sure he knew what he was saying. My new screen name would be Mitra Rohani.

Later that day, I signed the contract and received a check for one-third of the total I was to be paid. I left the production company with my first signed movie contract in my hand, holding it tightly as if it were the most precious thing in the world. I could not contain my happiness. I danced home with complete and utter joy. Little did I know that I might as well have been dancing on my grave.

Before arriving home, I had to come up with a way to break the news to my family. My father was out of the country on business. Although reasoning with my mother would be more challenging than with my father, I preferred that she be the one to give the news to him.

Heart pounding and preparing to lie, I turned the key in the lock, opened the door, and stepped into the house. My mother and Narine were drinking coffee in the living room. I hugged my mother and placed my check on the table in front of her.

She looked at it, and suddenly the expression on her face changed. She stood up, walked towards me with her gaze frozen as if penetrating my eyes in search of the truth. I stepped back not knowing what she was going to do. In this awkward situation, I heard her angry voice, "Where did this check come from, Linda?" She sounded worried.

I pulled every ounce of my strength together and dared to say, "Mom, I signed a movie contract, and this is the first installment of my salary."

My sister Narine pretended to be shocked, although she already knew. My mother, as if she could not believe her ears, asked, "What did you just say?"

She was making it difficult. Saying it once took all of my energy. Now she wanted me to repeat it. I looked at Narine for help, but she shrugged her shoulders, not wanting to get involved. I turned to my mother who was staring at me without blinking, waiting to hear once again what she was not prepared to hear.

Moving slowly away from her, I started to talk.

"Mom, I signed a contract to act in a movie. It is a big company, with so many famous actors. I did not know that I would be signing the contract today. Otherwise, I would have mentioned it to you beforehand."

Before I could do anything, my mother took the check from the table and tore it into pieces. Then she looked at me, pointing to the small pieces of my first big check and said, "You will cancel that contract before your father comes back. Afterward, we need to talk seriously about your understanding of this new-found independence."

"Mom, I can't withdraw now." I snapped. "If I cancel the contract, I have to pay a penalty of one million Tuman." This was a lie.

She cried out, almost screaming: "What, one million Tuman for cancellation of a contract? You said that you signed this damn contract a few hours ago, how can it not be canceled? If necessary, I will go there and cancel it myself and give them a piece of my mind, as well. Did you think about the fact that your parents would be against it? You knew by signing that contract you would put us in a situation where we could not come up with the million.

"Do you think because you've reached legal age, you can do whatever pleases you without any consideration for your family? This isn't acceptable at all, with your father or me. Speaking of your father, did you think about him when you signed that contract? Did you think about the anguish and torment you were going to cause him?"

I started to cry. My mother was accusing me of deliberately trying to hurt her and my father. That wasn't my intention. All I wanted was to act in movies. That's all.

Narine realized the situation was turning from bad to worse and spoke up, "Mom, why don't you talk to Dad and get his approval? You know the last word is yours. You can convince him. Linda always wanted to be on the stage, whether singing, modeling or acting. Now she has the opportunity, why do you make it such a big deal?"

Unfortunately, Narine's interference made the situation worse. Mom got angrier.

"Big deal, you think this is not a big deal? Are you with her in this? Linda knew we didn't want her to pursue a movie career. She knew she should not have signed that contract. How are we supposed to put a million together to cancel it?"

Turning her anger to me, she said, "You thought you were playing smart and safe? Well, it seems you have planned every step of your strategy. Tell me, what are your grand plans for facing your father about this?"

I cried out, "Mom please, I am not going to tell him any-thing, you do this, please, talk to him, just this once. I promise that next time I won't sign any paper without talking to you first. Please, Mom, I truly want this. Don't destroy my dreams."

Mom looked at me sternly and without another word, left the room clutching her coffee cup.

In the days that followed, I kept busy reading the screenplay and learning my part while anxiously awaiting Dad's return.

Mom kept her distance from me, hardly talking. A week later my father returned from his trip, and Mom performed a miracle. She told him the story and got his permission but under one condition.

"This should be her first and last movie."

I wish I could have heard her words. What kind of magic words did she use to convince my father to agree?

Four

The crew would shoot the first scenes in Abadan, the City of Oil. Abadan is in the southern part of Iran, with hot weather, oil pipelines, and refineries. Palm trees and colorful flowers beautified the streets.

The combination of the colors gave a unique appearance to the charming semi-western city despite the smell of crude oil that filled the air.

Most of the people who lived in the area, along with many others from foreign countries, worked for the National Iranian Oil Company. Oil was Iran's precious resource, generating many millions of dollars.

I checked into my hotel and relaxed in the beautifully decorated room, with its huge window opening to the street. I saw tall palm trees with branches like opened umbrellas. Some people were rushing around, others strolling along the sidewalk. The laughter of a few kids playing filled the whole street.

It was spring, the most beautiful and romantic season of the year. The sky seemed to whisper a sweet invitation to fall in love. I noticed a park on the corner. Under the shadow of an enormous palm tree, far from curious eyes of passersby, a young couple was sitting on a bench, kissing passionately.

My mind drifted to the last time a man had kissed me so tenderly. It was at sixteen, my first experience of love. I'd hid it from my parents.

My thoughts took me back to that time. My sister Narine was dating an Assyrian boy named Sammy. They were truly in love, and I could see how my sister was blossoming. Is this what love does to people? One afternoon, when Sammy and Narine were going to a tea dance at an Assyrian youth club, they invited me to join them.

The party was in a huge room. As I stood by the entrance, I could hear nearly everybody speaking Assyrian. I felt out of place as if I did not belong there. Though we all could speak Farsi, the Iranian national language, every minority had its own tongue.

Armenians spoke Armenian and Farsi; Assyrians spoke Assyrian and Farsi. I'd never been around a group of people whose spoken language was unfamiliar. I couldn't understand any of the conversation. Even Narine and Sammy would speak Farsi together, lacking the knowledge of each other's native language.

As I talked with them, a handsome boy came to our table. He introduced himself as Bernard, Sammy's brother. The two brothers spoke for a while, then, Bernard excused himself and left. I turned to Narine, "Sammy's brother is very cute," I said. "Why didn't you tell me anything about Bernard?"

Narine shrugged her shoulders, "I didn't think you would be interested."

"Don't you know that I am always interested in cute boys?" We laughed, and Narine went to dance.

Sitting at the table alone, I searched the room for a glimpse of Bernard. I saw him sitting with a group of people at a nearby table. I assumed the girl next to him was his girlfriend. Later I saw them holding hands walking to the dance floor. I thought, "What a waste," Bernard could do much better than that. I wondered what was wrong with me. Was I jealous?

A few days later, Narine told me that she was invited to Sammy's cousin's birthday party and asked me to go with them. Thinking that I might see Bernard again, I immediately accepted the invitation.

The evening of the party, Sammy picked us up a few blocks away from our home. We told our parents that we were going to a birthday party, but left out that it was not an Armenian gathering. Narine never wanted our parents to know her boyfriend was not Armenian.

After a short drive, we arrived in front of a beautiful mansion which was like nothing I had ever seen before. I felt like a queen as Sammy led us through the house into a large garden in the back.

"Come on," Sammy said, "I'll introduce you to everybody."

A tall girl with shiny blond hair smiled as we approached.

"Hello, Carol." Sammy said, "This is Narine, my girlfriend, and her sister, Linda. Girls, this is my cousin, Carol."

"Hello and welcome, I'm so glad you could come to my party," she said.

Sammy grabbed Narine's hand and took us both around the garden introducing us to the other guests.

"I'm hungry," Narine said, "let's get something to eat."

Canapés, caviar, all kinds of cold meats, assorted fruits, and cold drinks were laid out on several tables and being served by uniformed waiters. Narine grabbed at a big fat cherry and giggled as the sweet juice trickled down her chin.

"Mmmmm, this is so good. Try some Linda."

"Narine, be careful you are going to stain your dress," I said.

After mingling and being introduced to various people, Narine and Sammy headed hand-in-hand to the dance floor. The entire time, I did not see Bernard and thought he hadn't come.

The band was playing Tom Jones' "The Green, Green Grass of Home," a current hit in Tehran, and I loved it. As I closed my eyes, enjoying the melody and letting the music take over, I heard a voice.

"Hi Linda, I'm so glad you made it." It was Bernard. He was wearing beige slacks and a matching shirt.

I looked at him and answered. "I'm glad too."

He then held my hand as he asked, "Would you like to dance?" My hesitation did not go unnoticed by Bernard. Anxiously he asked, "Is there a problem? Are you here with somebody?"

I looked around instead of answering him. I was looking for his girlfriend, wondering why he wasn't dancing with her. "No, there is no problem," I answered. "Let's dance."

He put his arms around my waist, leading me to the dance floor. We got lost in the crowd and the music. It felt good to be in his arms. His after-shave smelled like cherry. I still remember. It was Old Spice. His hands around my waist, his face touching mine, gave me a strange-yet-wonderful feeling.

After the dance, we joined Narine and Sammy. One of the boys, whom I been introduced to earlier, approached our table and asked me for the next dance. While dancing with him, I saw Bernard and two of his other brothers, Frank and Harry, getting on the stage.

When Bernard started to play guitar and sing, his voice astounded me. The combination was heavenly. His voice was like velvet. Again, I looked around trying to see the girl I had assumed was dating him.

They played a few songs then left the stage. I don't know if it was his voice or guitar, but whatever it was, from that point on, I danced with no one else.

During a slow dance, Bernard pulled himself away, looked straight into my eyes, and said, "Can I ask you a personal question?"

I responded. "Well, it depends on how personal."

With a solemn look, he said, "Are you dating anyone? I mean, do you have a boyfriend?"

"No, I don't. I've never had one, but I think you have a girlfriend. I mean, the girl I saw you with last week at the tea dance. Isn't she your girlfriend?"

"No, she's not my girlfriend. We are just friends, nothing more. I've known her for a long time." Somehow, he did not sound convincing.

After that day we became inseparable.

Five

Friends were always welcome at our home, both girls and boys. My parents were at ease when they could keep an eye on us. However, when my mother found out that one of the so-called friends was my boyfriend, and he was not an Armenian, she told my father about my relationship.

On one of Tehran's hot summer evenings, I was in my room with Narine chatting, listening to music and having fun when Edwin came in and said: "Hey, Linda, Dad wants to see you."

In the living room, Mom and Dad were sitting together on the couch. My father looked straight at me, sparks of anger darkened his hazel and usually kind eyes. His cold voice broke the heavy silence:

"I will not let him even carry your dead body in your coffin on his shoulders."

I looked at my dad, puzzled. What was he saying? He continued, "I have nothing more to say. You have disappointed me beyond words. Don't look at me so innocently. Go to your room."

I went back to my room still trying to understand my father's anger and harsh words. He had never spoken to me in that tone or used words like that. I had tears in my eyes. I was hurt, heartbroken, and confused. He rarely spoke to us with even a cold tone.

Narine was sitting on her bed; she looked at me but said nothing. She'd heard what Dad had said and known why. She realized that I didn't understand, and I wanted her to explain my father's harsh words.

"He knows about your relationship," she said.

So, Dad was talking about my boyfriend. He'd meant Bernard wasn't even worthy to carry my dead body. I knew exactly why; he was not Armenian.

It was a great dishonor for Armenians when their sons or daughters had relationships outside their culture, especially if their choice in partner wasn't Christian, a minority in Iran. But Bernard was Christian.

The biggest nightmare for Armenian parents was that their daughters might fall in love with, or worse, marry a Muslim. I knew the community judged such girls harshly. Somehow, they more quickly forgave Armenian boys who did the same.

The root of this attitude went back to 1915 when the Turks massacred one and a half million Armenians. My father used to read to us about the genocide.

He was an infant when his father rushed home, took his family and ran away because the Turks were so close, my grandfather had little time to gather belongings. There was only enough time to take his wife and children and flee, not knowing to where.

The Turks butchered many and raped women and girls, then tortured and killed them. Thousands of survivors were scattered all over the world. My family ended up in Iran.

But why be against Bernard? I still couldn't grasp it. Why was my family rejecting a Christian who believed as we did? He was Assyrian and Catholic.

According to my parents' beliefs, inherited from their ancestors, Armenians should marry Armenians and re-populate so that they continue to exist as a nation.

After my father's to-the-point warning, I had no choice but to keep my relationship with Bernard a secret. At times, I had to beg Narine to cover for me so I could see him. Narine, being more clever, never invited Sammy to our house.

A few months later, Narine and Sammy broke-up, making it difficult for Bernard and me to see each other as much since he would come along when Sammy came to see my sister.

I enjoyed spending time with him and listening to his music. I loved his kisses and his voice so much. I was in love and so happy to be with him, my first love. I wanted to marry him.

One afternoon, after watching a movie at a theater, Bernard suggested we go to a nearby park for a walk. All the way to the park, he was unusually quiet.

Man-made ponds, waterfalls, colorful flowers and beautiful plants filled the park. Birds were singing, couples were strolling hand in hand, and a few children were cheerfully running around under watchful eyes of their parents.

As we sat on a bench, Bernard lit a cigarette and put his arm around my shoulder. I couldn't wait any longer and asked, "What's wrong, Babe? You look far away as if you aren't here. Talk to me. What's the matter?"

His eyes filled with tears as he said, "My parents have decided to move our family to Sidney, Australia. Last night my father told us. My brothers and I are strongly against the idea, but we have no choice. My Dad is going to sell the house and the business, and we are leaving Iran forever."

He was still talking, but I was not hearing him. My ears were burning. It was as if my heart stopped. The horror of the news and losing Bernard made me momentarily deaf.

The only thing I could hear was the sound of my heart breaking. Looking at him in horror, I tried to talk, but words were meaningless.

Finally, I managed to ask, "When are you leaving?"

"I think in about two months," he replied. "I still can't believe I only have two more months with the love of my life."

He started to cry.

Just a couple of months? His move sounded like exile. We knew we couldn't change anything. All we could do was hold on to the time we had left.

However, during those precious two months, the strangest thing happened, something that changed my whole idea about men and love.

One afternoon, after shopping with my mother, we hailed a cab to go home. On the way, we passed the theater where Bernard and I frequently saw movies. Suddenly I saw Bernard and a girl walking towards it. I saw him from behind, but I was sure it was him.

I could distinguish him from among ten thousand men. I didn't have time to look again. I couldn't stop the cab and run after him. Even if so, what could I do? Yell, "I caught you!"

My heart broke. At that moment the most precious feelings I had for him, respect and trust, were destroyed.

I was fuming but unable to confront him from inside the cab with my mother. How I wanted to look into his lying eyes. I cursed myself for not having made up an excuse to stop the taxi. Now, it was too late.

When we arrived home, I immediately called Bernard, but Sammy answered. After the usual greetings, I asked to talk to Bernard.

Sammy said, "He's not here. He's at band practice. I'll tell him to call you when he gets home."

Of course, he wasn't home. I knew he was with another girl at "our" movie theater, cheating on me during our last weeks together. How could he?

Foolishly, I tried to convince myself it was a mistake. From behind, how could I be sure it was him? Was I foolish to consider such a thing? No, I was not foolish. I knew the jacket he wore and I had seen him with my own eyes. I knew I was right. It was Bernard, and the girl was Irene. I had seen her before.

I remembered one night at a disco where Bernard's band was playing. She had approached me, while I was dancing with Harry, Bernard's brother. She asked, "Is Harry your boyfriend or Bernard?" Her question seemed intrusive.

I replied, "Why do you want to know?"

She smiled saying, "No particular reason."

I replied, "Bernard is my boyfriend."

When she heard my response, she turned toward Bernard and gave him a dirty look as if to say, "You liar!" Then she left.

I asked Harry if he knew her. He said, "Yes. Her name is Irene, a regular."

Soon I forgot all about Irene, and Bernard and I continued to spend as much time as possible together.

However, after the movie incident, something new was born in me. I came to believe men were not to be trusted and would eventually all cheat, regardless of how beautiful or faithful their girlfriend is.

Furious when Bernard called, I controlled myself and didn't mention that I had seen him with another girl. Knowing he was not what I had thought and that he was leaving soon, I figured there was no point in telling him he had lost his place in my heart.

Of course, I was no angel. I would flirt now and then, but I never crossed the line. If I had stopped that damn cab and confronted him immediately, I wouldn't be in this situation. Maybe he had cheated many times before, and now the truth was out.

Blaming Bernard for cheating was breaking my heart. What if I was wrong? Though I had always trusted him, my inner voice was helping me to believe what I had to believe.

It was late evening when he finally called. "Hi, Beautiful, Sammy said you called and didn't sound your usual. What's the matter? I was practicing all day with the band and just got home. Calling you was the first thing on my mind. I miss you like crazy."

Was he lying? Why didn't I stop the cab? Then I would know for certain. "What sort of instrument were you playing today?"

"What do you mean?" Bernard asked, puzzled.

Almost shouting, I told him what I had seen that day, and if it had not been for my mother, I would have stopped the car and confronted him.

Bernard sounded shocked, "How on earth can you be this cruel?" You know you are the only girl in my life. Why are you doing this to us? Don't we have enough to worry about right now?"

I said, "I'm not crazy. You were with someone I saw at the club where you play, taking her to the same theater where you take me. I could recognize you from a mile away. If I had not been with my mother, I would have ruined your date. How could you do this to me?"

"Just give me one reason why I would cheat on you, Linda. You are all I want, and that's it." He said that I had imagined things and wished I had stopped the car to get a better look at the person I thought was him.

Now I was confused, wanting to think I might have been wrong, but, I felt a certainty.

Because he was leaving soon, I forced thoughts of him cheating out of my head. After a week, we didn't even talk about it anymore, but the incident created an ugly and merciless monster of revenge in me.

Eventually, the day Bernard was to leave had arrived. Our parting was bitter and sad. I still remember his face, his last words, and the tender goodbye kisses. At the airport, we both cried during our last moments together. It hurt tremendously.

He kept promising that soon after his arrival in Sydney he would find a job, save money, and send me a ticket to join him. After our bitter final goodbye, he got on the bus to the plane. Standing at the back window crying, he stared out at me. That moment would be the last time I saw him.

A few weeks later, I received a letter from him describing how much he loved and missed me, he was making plans, and anticipating when we would be together. The last lines repeated the words "I love you." I responded in kind, saying I was waiting to join him.

I received five such letters. In the fifth, instead of his usual repeating of "I love you," he wrote, "Do you think I don't know what you are doing there without me?"

What? What on earth was he saying? Of course, I was going to parties and the disco but was remaining faithful. I was so angry that I didn't respond.

To my great surprise, I never received another letter from Bernard. He did not even write to tell me it was over or give reasons.

A few months after Bernard's insulting final letter, I started to date again. This time I didn't allow any man to capture my heart and always kept an escape route. I would do the choosing, pursue him, get him, then right when he would fall in love, I would leave.

I remember my first New Year's Eve after Bernard. I accepted invitations to parties from two different boys. They arrived at the same time to pick me up. The three of us spent the night at two different parties.

I had fun dancing the night away but didn't even bother to get to know them. Strangely enough, deep down in my heart, I guess I still loved Bernard and was punishing others for his betrayal.

This was to be my new way with men.

Six

A knock shattered my reverie. Back in the present, I opened the door to find Bijan in a casual summer outfit.

"Hi Linda, let's go join the crew for lunch," he said.

After lunch, Saied, our director, came to my room with the screenplay, explaining my role and giving me useful instruction. "Tomorrow, early in the morning, we will go to a nearby semi-island called Minoo for shooting," he said.

It was happening! Tomorrow the cameras would roll, and I would act in my first movie. My dream was mine to have. That evening, I did some shopping and sightseeing. Not yet famous, I was free to stroll from place to place, all the while excited to become an actress.

The next morning, after a quick breakfast, with a caravan of cars, equipment, and people, we drove to Minoo Island. My excitement was mixed with fear. I was in a movie, but could I act? My reality was no longer just a dream. Was I good enough to do this?

Bijan was standing close by. As if noticing my fears, he approached me and put his hands around my shaking shoulders.

Looking straight into my eyes he said, "Everything is going to be all right. Don't worry. I will help you. Don't think about acting. Think of it as if you are a storyteller, and this is your story to tell. Give life to the story, and make it yours. Go on, show them what you can do."

When the set was ready, I heard the click of the camera and the director's voice shouting, "Action!" Strangely enough, my fear was gone.

In one of the scenes we were shooting, Bijan had to kiss me. His kisses felt real and passionate as if he were not acting. Was he that good of an actor that he could make his kiss feel so real, or was he actually kissing me?

After shooting for hours, the camera finally went silent. Everyone cheered. I had done it. Saied came to me, gave me a big hug and announced loudly, "Today a star is born!"

When everything was packed, we drove back to the mainland. Delirium saturated the car's air. Everyone talked, sang, and told jokes. Bijan was sitting next to me, silent.

At the hotel, before everyone left for their rooms, our producer announced that we were going to have a party that night to celebrate the start of the movie. He had invited local celebrities, too.

When I got to my room, I jumped on my bed, kicking into the air, telling myself, "Well, Linda, now you are an actress. Today was the start of your journey to the world of movies and entertainment."

Seven

The party started around eight o'clock that night; anyone who was anyone in the movies crowded the ballroom. Big band music played to a packed dance floor from a huge stage, decorated to reflect the festive evening. As I watched couples moving to the rhythm of the music, our director Saied came rushing toward me with a big grin.

"You look astonishing...no, breathtaking, Linda. You're the most beautiful girl I have ever seen," he said. I laughed at his exaggeration as he led me straight to the dance floor; we started to sway to the music. I saw Bijan sitting at a table with the producer and cameraman, surrounded by a group of women, each competing for Bijan's attention.

When the music stopped, Saied and I joined them at their table. I tried not to get close to Bijan, although I wanted to; he was a very handsome man. A voice inside me kept repeating, "He's married."

"Would you like to dance?" It was Bijan, standing next to me, his hand raised toward me. I looked at him, then, at the envious faces of the women who were there. "Yes, I'd love too," I answered.

Holding hands, we walked toward the dance floor. The band was playing one of the season's hits, a Farsi love song called "Ice Flower." Bijan held me gently but tightly. His cologne smelled of fresh lemon or a pine tree after a heavy rain. We didn't talk; we just danced. I let him and the music lead me. The others in the room faded from my mind until I could see and hear only the two of us. The voice inside repeated, "He's married."

When the music stopped, he walked me to my seat, thanked me for the dance, and left. A few minutes later, I saw him carrying two drinks as he walked toward our table. He offered me one, raised his glass, and said. "A toast! To a very beautiful and talented young lady. Welcome to the fascinating world of movies."

He turned to Saied and said, "She is not only a good actor but a great dancer, is she not?" Then he bent over my shoulders and whispered in my ear. "You look wonderful tonight." I saw the admiration in his eyes and the ring on his finger.

I spent the rest of the evening dancing with our crew, but mostly with Bijan, enjoying the envious, disappointed faces of jealous women.

It was late when I returned to my room and opened the window, feeling the night's cool breeze on my skin. Stars were shining, and the moon was peaceful and romantic.

As I lay down, my thoughts went to Bijan. He was very kind, gentle, articulate, handsome, famous...and married. Stories of his affairs with other women and his co-stars were everywhere. I alternated between pleasure and guilt for the rest of the night.

As the days quickly passed, Bijan and I became closer. We would spend our free time together. He told me of his life, and how unhappy he was.

Then, the day came to shoot the final scene. We were to swim out to sea, reach a waiting boat, jump into it, and cross the border before my character's father, who was chief of police, could arrest Bijan's character, a murderer running from the law, with whom my character had fallen in love.

While we were escaping, my "father" would shoot him from the shore, just a few miles before freedom. He would die in my arms. Total silence would follow, except for the sound of my hysterical cries and frightened seabirds flapping their wings.

"Cut, cut," the director yelled in excitement.

In the boat, Bijan was still laying in my arms with false blood coming out of his chest. It felt so real that my father had killed the man I loved. I cried until Bijan opened his eyes, sat up straight, and teased me saying, "Don't cry, I'm not dead," he laughed, standing to take the wheel.

When our boat reached the shore, Saied gave me a hug and said, "It is unbelievable, your acting is just great, you are going to become a big name."

Bijan stood next to me and said, "I'm proud of you. It was a great pleasure to have you as my co-star." He gave me a hug and a kiss on my cheek.

As the shooting wrapped, Bijan and I began a relationship. I struggled to ignore the constant voice inside my head, but it wouldn't leave me alone. "He's married," it kept reminding me. I had never dated a married man. What was wrong with me? Was I turning into a sinner?

Before the movie's release, almost everyone in the industry knew something had developed between Bijan and me.

Several newspapers wrote articles about the movie and our forbidden love. In a magazine, I saw a picture of us with an article saying, "Bijan and Mitra are burning in the flames of forbidden love." It continued, "Bijan is a Muslim and Mitra, a Christian."

Privacy was impossible. Every movement was illustrated in the magazines the next day. The situation was impossible. I could not have a relationship with a Muslim and let it be known to the world.

My behavior was going to backfire on my family and me. How on earth did I dare to go against our tradition? The reporters, hungry for a story, especially if it was scandalous, were going to shadow us and write about my every anti-traditional move.

"He won't even carry your dead body," were my father's words when he found out about Bernard, my Assyrian Christian boyfriend. How would he react to this forbidden relationship?

However, I didn't give a damn about what others thought or said. I lied to my family again, telling them, "The press will write lies just to promote the movie so that people come to see it. These kinds of stories will appear whenever I act in a movie."

Back in Tehran, Bijan and I continued to date but always tried to avoid reporters and the public eye. Hidden from scrutiny, we were happy, chatting, laughing, eating, drinking and making love.

Eight

Soon, I signed my second contract. When I told Bijan, he became angry. He didn't want me to appear in films in which he had no part. For me, it was a new world full of discovery. I wanted to perform, with or without Bijan. I loved my career. I was not going to give it up just because he was unhappy.

Within a week of the second movie wrapping, I had signed onto my third, in which Bijan also was starring. The shooting was in mid-summer in the city of Jahrom to take advantage of its historical settings.

When shooting finished, we returned to Tehran. For some time, I didn't hear from Bijan. He didn't call. We didn't see each other until shooting resumed in Tehran. During those few weeks, I had time to think about our affair.

Though Bijan was married, I missed him, but my relentless inner voice became louder: *"He's married. He is married."*

We met again on set. Seeing him after almost a month, my whole body trembled with excitement. My breath left me when we said hello and shook hands.

The crew was busy preparing for shooting. I left the set, walking aimlessly for half an hour, trying to still the voice and gather my thoughts. Upon returning to the waiting cast, the sound of the camera pulled me out of my misery.

Despite the voice's warnings, our relationship picked up from where it had been. Bijan said he didn't call or stay in touch because he was battling the reality of his life and the love he felt for me. He said he thought he would forget about me, just as he had forgotten his other affairs, but this was different.

He admitted he was madly in love and that it was impossible for him not to be with me. He wanted to spend the rest of his life with me.

The rest of his life! My dream career was just starting. I considered him my boyfriend and enjoyed his company, but wasn't willing to give it all up at any price. I was too young for long term plans, let alone marriage. But then I thought, maybe I'm wrong, maybe he is not talking about marriage.

Meanwhile, I started to have problems with my parents. They didn't approve of my career and wanted me to give it up, go to Europe to continue my education, and after that, marry a decent Armenian.

Despite disapproval from my parents and Bijan, I started my fourth and fifth films, Bijan wanted to limit my acting to movies in which he would be lead male and asked me to refuse offers. I didn't like the idea of becoming a movie couple and didn't want to limit my career opportunities.

Meanwhile, Bijan filed for divorce for a second time. He and his wife had divorced and then remarried a couple of years later. Slowly, he started to talk to me about marriage. Even though our relationship continued to be passionate, something else began to creep into it, and it made me uncomfortable.

Bijan was becoming jealous and possessive. He started to control my movie contracts, even deciding which I should accept and which I should reject. He didn't want anyone else to touch or kiss me, even in the movies.

I loved him and didn't want to upset him, but I loved my way of life, too, and my career. He was my boyfriend, not my agent or mentor. I didn't want him controlling me. No one had ever dared to do that. Hadn't I dreamed my whole life of becoming an actress? Why should I let him end the dream now that I had achieved it?

The situation would soon become more impossible. One night after dinner and a movie, we went to his place. While Bijan went to change, I searched the radio dial for mood music and waited on the sofa. Carrying two glasses and a bottle of red wine, he sat next to me, kicked his shoes off, and leaned back.

From chatting about ordinary things, our conversation turned to my former boyfriends, with Bijan claiming none of them loved me as he did. In particular, he hated my last boyfriend, without even knowing him.

We began arguing about the past. He walked to the bar to make a scotch and ice. I could see he was drinking too much. While sipping his drink, he remarked that my ex-boyfriend was a jerk who had only wanted sex.

His words irritated and hurt me. I snapped back, "For your information, women enjoy sex as much as men. Maybe I enjoyed it more than he did."

I had hardly finished my sentence when, suddenly, he jumped at me, held my face in his hands and bit my upper lip so hard that it started to bleed. I was stunned and could hardly register what had happened. The hot blood running from my lip shook me to the bitter reality of what he had done.

Ignoring my need for medical attention, he dialed the phone. I somehow knew he was calling his brothers. Hanging up, he walked toward me with a glassy glare. Never had I felt such fear. He grabbed my hand, pulled me away from the sofa, dragged me to his car and said, "I will show you and that bastard who enjoyed it the most."

I was horrified. Instead of tending to me and grasping what he'd done, he totally ignored my injury and began driving like a maniac, to where I had no idea. Trying to stop the bleeding, I realized for the first time I was afraid of him and was shaking in terror.

Instead of taking me to a clinic, Bijan drove to the discotheque where my ex-boyfriend performed. My upper lip, cut and severely swollen, had bled onto my clothes. Knowing he was about to start a fight, I felt helpless and embarrassed to be with him in public. In that moment, I realized the truth: my boyfriend was psychotic.

His brothers were waiting at the entrance. The four of us entered the club, where despite the darkness, people noticed us.

Fortunately, my ex wasn't there. Thank God Bijan's plan didn't work. As we were leaving, I thought he might take me to the emergency room, but he took me to my house.

On the way, he became apologetic, crying and begging for forgiveness. He blamed his crazy behavior on his deep love for me, saying that the thought of someone else touching me drove him insane. Not speaking a word, I just wanted to get out of that car and out of his life. I planned never to see his face again.

I prayed God would not let my family see me in this terrifying condition. They would be shocked and scandalized.

Fortunately, it was late, and they were asleep. I desperately needed time to come up with a logical explanation for my injury. The bleeding had stopped, but I looked like a boxer who had lost a match. My lip was swollen and torn. How would I face my family in the morning?

Lying in bed, I began to cry. The salty tears stung my injured lip, and my mouth felt like it was on fire. I sat up, looking for water. I could not leave my room. Any sound might wake my family, and I was not ready to face them.

In the darkness, I found a bottle of water and soothed my lip. I couldn't tell how severe the injury was and wondered if it would heal or look scarred or deformed. Could I go out in public or to movie studios? Above all, I wondered how I would get rid of Bijan.

No man had ever dared be rough with me, let alone cause injury. I had no experience with domestic violence. Frightened, I felt that I genuinely hated him. Remembering the pain of my burning lip stopped me from crying further. Instead, I felt angry at myself for allowing Bijan to lower me to this level. The relationship was over. All I felt for him now was hate and fear.

Nine

On the verge of insanity, my head spinning, I didn't have time to agonize over my pain. I was preoccupied with how I was going to face my family in just a few hours. The horror of my situation overwhelmed me. Sobbing, I buried my face in my pillow and wished to die. For the first time in my life, humiliation shattered my soul.

The emotions were unbearable. Hands that were supposed to soothe had hurt me. Lips, to kiss, had attacked me. This was not love. I could recall love; I had it long ago.

Finally, the night gave way to morning. Still awake, I had been unable to invent a story to explain my injury.

Narine cried out. She had awoken and seen my face. Horrified, with eyes wide open in terror, she threw her hands over her mouth, stifling a scream. Her reaction made me hide my face in my pillow. I didn't want to scare her.

She came closer, sat next to me, and gently removed the pillow from my hands. Looking at my face, she started to cry. Her crying made me start crying again. Once more, the salty tears reached my lip, and a burning sensation went through my whole face. Holding me tightly in her arms, Narine was caressing my hair, then the questions began.

"Linda, what happened to your lip?"

"When did you come home?"

"Why didn't you wake me up?"

"Let me look at your face, oh, dear Lord, look at this wound."

"How did you manage to screw up your lip like this?"

"Where were you?"

"Have you been to the emergency room?"

"Who brought you home?"

I saw a thousand more questions in her brown eyes, but I didn't know what to say. Even to her, from whom I never kept secrets, I was unable to tell the truth.

Still lost in thought, I heard her say, "If this happened on the set while working, you know what Dad will say this time. Do you remember what he said when you came home with a bleeding nose?"

Yes, I remembered. My father had said, "If I see you harmed one more time while shooting a movie, I will make sure it's your last film. I don't want to worry all the time that something horrible might happen on the set."

My heart leaped. Of course, why had I not thought of it? Narine had given me my cover. This happened on the set. Was this brilliant idea going to save me? It might, but given my father's ultimatum, it would mean the end of my acting career.

I started to beg God to show me the way. If my parents were to see my face, my mother would collapse, and my father would make sure that I never stood in front of another camera.

Narine's voice interrupted my thoughts, "Here, put this ice on your lip." With a bitter smile, she continued, "You look like a boxer who has been knocked out." I started to cry.

"No, no, don't cry, please, that wasn't meant to hurt you, I just wanted to say something funny to make you laugh." She sat next to me, holding me tightly in her arms, together we cried.

Finally, I managed to talk. "Narine, I can't let Mom and Dad see my face. They will pass out. I am in so much pain that my brain is not working. I look like a monster." But the real monster was the one who did this to me.

"Just stay in bed, I'll tell them you have a headache and are still sleeping."

"Narine, do you think this is going to leave a scar?"

She looked at me with surprise and said, "Let's worry about keeping Mom and Dad away from you, then we'll see how your wound is healing."

When she left the room, I pulled the blanket over my head in case my mother came in.

I woke up to Narine's voice. "Linda, Linda, are you asleep? Are you okay?"

I sprang straight up, frightened. "What's wrong?" I asked frantically. "Do they know what's happened? Has anyone seen me?"

"No, don't worry," she said. She was looking at me strangely. She held my shoulders gently, saying "You are the luckiest girl I've ever seen."

I was puzzled. She continued. "Dad left town for a week. During breakfast, I heard him telling Mom that he was not happy to leave early but the trip would be short."

With a sigh of relief, I thanked God for His mercy.

Later that day, when my mother saw my face, she almost fainted. Narine and I told her that somehow, I had lost my balance, fell and hurt my lip when it hit the corner of the desk in our room before I hit the floor.

My lip began to heal, but the wound on my soul was a permanent reminder of Bijan's animal behavior and sickening love. Thankfully, he kept his distance.

He was the most contradictory person I had ever met. He would give so much that no one else could compete, yet he could take so much out of me. Being afraid of him was very strange; a first for me in any relationship.

For the next while, I stayed home as much as I could, wanting to avoid having to explain what had happened to my face. I spent time thinking about possible new movies to act in, avoiding Bijan in any of them.

Listening to music and going through pictures from a film set, I yearned to return to work in front of the camera. Busy in my thoughts, I absentmindedly answered the phone when no one was home. It was Bijan! I almost dropped the receiver.

"Hi Linda, it's me. How is my beautiful flower? I can't wait to see you. I miss you. Sorry, I couldn't call for a while, I was away filming at different sites. What about you?"

I wasn't expecting to hear his voice again. I was speechless. Most shocking, he pretended that nothing had happened. He didn't even ask how my lip was or about my wounded heart and shattered pride.

He didn't even bother to apologize for the humiliation he put me through. There would be no forgiving him for what he had done to me in the name of "love."

Shamelessly, he continued. "I have a surprise for you, Honey. I have reserved a room at your favorite hotel at the Caspian Sea for a week. We leave in two days, so get ready to have a great time, Babe."

He was talking as if everything was normal, and we were the happiest couple in the world. It was incomprehensible. How could he dare to call, let alone invite me to vacation with him? It was as if he had amnesia.

I finally managed to speak. "Why are you calling me? How dare you! I don't want to see your face or hear your voice ever again. You are dead to me, yet you call to go on vacation? Have you lost your mind? It's over. Don't you dare call me ever again!"

For the first time, I was not afraid of him. Perhaps my sudden bravery was because of the safe distance between us.

I continued: "I hate you for what you've done. Stay away from me. You are a monster. Leave me alone you sick son of a bitch."

There was silence, and then I heard his voice, sounding cold and brutal.

"If you don't go with me, I will send some sexy photos to your father so he can see what sort of a daughter he has."

I felt a million volts of electricity shoot through my body. Breathing became almost impossible, as all the air left my lungs. My heart was pounding, my ears were whistling, and my mouth soured. A cold shiver went down my spine.

I remembered the pictures, taken some months ago at his place when he was showing me his new Polaroid camera. I had never seen one and found it amazing that it required no lab to develop the photos.

He began to shoot photos, saying they would be for his eyes only and comfort him when we were apart. In one, I was topless but trusted that my boyfriend, whom I thought adored me, would be the only one to see it.

I had forgotten all about the photos. Now, I cursed myself a thousand times for letting him take them. What would be his next move, sending them to the magazines and newspapers?

He knew very well that there was no price I wouldn't pay to keep the pictures and our relationship hidden from my family. There would be no way I could look into my parent's eyes again, especially my father's. I sensed Bijan meant what he was saying. He was going to force a relationship. Why would he want to be with someone who didn't want him?

Feeling I had no choice, I packed and went on holiday with him. Or more accurately, I went to serve my sentence. I had to find those pictures.

Ten

The holiday I was dreading soon arrived. From the moment he arrived to pick me up, he worked hard to make amends. Time after time, he promised he would never hurt me again, saying, "I love you very much and cannot tolerate the image of you being with other men. Life without you has no meaning for me."

Why was the past so important to him? It made no sense. Not being the first woman in his life had not bothered me at all.

During the trip, I could have asked for the stars. He turned into the man I had wanted him to be. Instead of being afraid of him, I started to love and trust him again. I forgave him. It seemed no one could love me the way he did. No one had ever been so madly in love with me. But did I need mad love?

Soon after, our relationship had returned to normal. It seemed he had realized how wrong he had been to cause such hurt. He would repeatedly mention that I was the most precious thing in his life.

When we had free time, we would spend it together at his place. On one of those carefree days, after we had had sex, he sat straight up and said, "Linda, I want to ask your Dad for his permission to marry you."

My heart sank; my whole body went numb.

I knew the first word that should have come was, "No." But I was scared to speak. I sensed the explosion that would follow if I did. I couldn't go through being hurt again, so I said nothing. My thoughts went back to the night he had bitten my lip.

Knowing my father would likely say, "Over my dead body," gave me some comfort. He may even ask him to leave and never set foot in our house again. But afterward, facing my dad to explain the situation would be another story. My parents would exile me.

The evening came. Bijan was at my home, asking my father, who looked surprised, if they could talk in private. I played dumb and waited in my room. The conversation was short. I came out to see Bijan, with a grim look on his face, headed toward the door, motioning that he would be waiting in his car.

A few minutes later my brother summoned, "Dad wants to see you."

I knew what my father would say. Pretending not to know Bijan's intention would be the role of my life. But Dad was not a director or producer. He was my father and could read me better than anyone else. I pulled myself together, needing an academy award performance.

Standing by a window smoking a cigarette, Dad motioned me to sit, then asked; "Did you know why he came here to talk in private?" I just shook my head, trying to stay calm. He looked at me with an unforgettable expression of disdain.

"That idiot was asking for my permission to marry you," he snapped, angrily.

I tried to look shocked. "What? Has he lost his mind? This is nonsense, Dad. I will tell him to stop dreaming."

Again, one of those looks. He kept quiet for a while and then continued, "I think it is time for you to leave the country. I'm sending you to Europe."

He paused for a second, looking straight into my eyes so he could tell if I was lying, just as he did when I was a child. Always, either the right or the left eye, one of the two, we never knew which, would alert him if any of us kids were lying.

He said, "Why don't you reconsider the scholarship from Talar Roodaki and go to Vienna? You've always loved music. Frankly, I also like music better than acting. Don't forget that your mother and I could visit from time to time."

"But Dad, I already refused that long ago; I don't want to live away from my family."

He paid no attention, but said, "I will talk to your mother when she comes back."

My mother and my sister, Anais, were in Armenia visiting my mother's family. Mom had not been there for many years. "By the way," my father added, "I will be traveling in a couple of weeks. By the time I get back, your mother will be home too. We will decide then."

While leaving the house, I glanced at Dad's face. His hazel eyes did not have their natural shine. They were dull and sad with obvious concern and tears. It broke my heart and my entire being.

ꙮ

Bijan, still in his car, was smoking a cigarette. I got in, and we didn't speak for a while, both drowning in our thoughts. Looking over, I noticed his face glistening with tears. Both of the men in my life were in tears tonight.

With a long sigh and broken voice, Bijan said "Your father threw a big 'No!' at me and refused to even let me finish. He said there is no way I can marry you. He planned to send you to Europe and suggested I find someone who would suit me better. I think he meant a Muslim woman. Linda, I swear to God, there would not be anyone else. I love you. If you don't marry me, I will die. I will kill myself. I love you, and I know you love me too, marry me please."

He was in my arms crying like a child. I couldn't stand it and joined him in tears. "Don't worry," I said, "We will find a way. All we need is time." I knew I didn't need time. I needed a way out of marriage.

He finally drove off. In my room, cursing myself for creating this mess, I wallowed in regret. I should not have had an affair with a married man. Now I was being punished for my indecent mistake.

Bijan had asked me to move into his place the day my father left the country and immediately get married.

When we first started dating, I didn't even think about a long-term relationship. I was young. Every girl my age was dating and had a boyfriend. I wanted to continue to live however I wanted to. I was not ready to marry anyone, let alone Bijan. I was too young for that. Still, I didn't have the guts to tell him that I'd rather date him than to marry him.

Throughout my short life, I had never underestimated myself or thought I would be easily intimidated, but here I was, acting like a scared mouse.

Soon my father left for Europe. I wished that he could have stayed. It was the worst time to go away. I wished I could tell my dad about my worries and ask him not to go.

I kept the news from Bijan. I needed time to think. As long as Bijan didn't know about my father's absence, time would be on my side. I was desperately looking for a way out; I did not want to marry yet.

Only four months ago, I had turned twenty-one, not an age I considered ideal for marriage, particularly to someone like Bijan.

I didn't know what my next step would be. Deep down, I knew love wasn't keeping us together. It was the power of fear. I have never been so fearful of anyone in my life, not even my father. I knew any wrong step could put me in danger. I always wanted the man in my life to love me more than I loved him, but not like this. His love was dangerous and suffocating. He believed that if he couldn't have me, then no one could.

With both my parents out of the country, I had no one to turn to and no place to hide. I still loved Bijan, but not enough to marry him. Then, two weeks later, Bijan found out that my father had left. One evening, he called to say that he would pick me up around eight to go to dinner and would wait at the corner so my dad wouldn't see him.

"Don't worry about that; my dad's out of town." In a fraction of a second, I realized my mistake. Those words destroyed my plan; now I'd have to deal with the consequences.

"When did your father leave? Why didn't you tell me?" Bijan bombarded me with questions in a very demanding tone.

"He left this afternoon; I forgot to mention it." I lied, still cursing myself for being my worst enemy.

Soon, one hot summer afternoon, Bijan came to pick me up for good.

8)❦(C3

I will never forget the day I left what had been my home for so many years. Every corner of the house was witness to the happiness I felt while living there with my family. It was painful to know I would no longer be part of the family that loved and protected me. I wished I could stand up for myself and not let him intimidate me.

I had to start packing. Bijan sat on my bed watching with pleasure as I cut the ties to my past. Like a robot, I threw things into the suitcase that I didn't even need. It was as if leaving my important things would find me back home again, where I belonged.

I managed to hide Bernard's letters in the suitcase. I would read them occasionally. Taking them was asking for trouble, but worth the risk. He had been my first love. Bernard had too much self-respect to keep me in his life by force. If Bernard had stayed, things would be very different right now. Subconsciously, I was blaming Bernard for my entrapment.

Bijan was excited, happy, laughing and telling jokes. I wished I could be as happy, but my heart was crying. Leaving the nest where I had been shielded for so long to step into an unknown future was devastating.

What had happened to my tongue? Why couldn't I tell Bijan I didn't want to leave my home, and I did not want to marry? I started to hate myself for not standing up for what I thought was right.

He carried my suitcase to his car and put it in the trunk. Sitting next to him, I looking at our house for the last time. The living room windows opened to the street, where my dad liked to sit, drinking his evening tea, reading the newspaper and chatting with my mother. I pictured our cozy kitchen, where my mom created miracles with her fantastic cooking. I thought of my room, where Narine and I shared many late nights and long talks. Leaving this haven, I knew it would be impossible to return.

Bijan started the engine, pressed the clutch, first gear, second gear, slowly moving away from my past. That is how I left home, ending that chapter of my life.

During the next few weeks, Bijan was busy organizing our wedding. He even instructed me to have an interview announcing my departure from films. The article read, "Mitra Rohani announces she is leaving the movie world to marry Bijan Valayati."

Colleagues were shocked at the news. They knew we were dating, but my marrying Bijan caught them by surprise. Some called to warn me not to marry him. They said my future in the movies was bright, that I should not throw it away.

Eleven

Our wedding ceremony, followed by a party, took place on a hot summer evening in June of 1974 at Bijan's house.

I had gone to buy my dress only the day before. As I was trying on the first gown, I looked at myself in the mirror. It was a cute white gown but on the wrong person.

I wondered why I didn't have that feeling of enormous excitement expected of any bride. After all, it was my wedding; happening only once in a lifetime, but nothing even close to the description of the excitement of other brides was in my heart.

Around noon on the day of the wedding, I went to the salon for hair and makeup. As soon as the stylist washed my hair, I felt there was no reason to be coiffed. I asked her just to wash and brush my hair, and in an hour I was done. It was time for this bride to go to her wedding.

While sitting in the back seat of a cab on the way to Bijan's house, the thought of fleeing overtook me. I could go somewhere to hide until everyone forgot about me, in particular, Bijan. I knew this, too, was a pipe dream.

Bijan would not let go that easily and would find me anywhere I went. He was capable of harming my family, too. I felt like the saddest bride in the world. I couldn't feel the slightest shred of happiness in my heart.

Bijan had decided to invite only those closest to us to the wedding. From my side, my sister, Narine, and brother, Edwin were present. I had begged them both not to leave me alone on that day. They didn't want to come; no one from my family liked Bijan.

From Bijan's family, his father and two brothers were present. The rest of the guests consisted of some hand-picked people from the movie industry along with very few of Bijan's friends. A reporter and photographer from a movie magazine completed the list of attendees.

A Mullah or Islamic clergy performed the wedding that evening on what should have been the happiest day of my life. Instead, it felt like a lost day. The words, "I do," sounded empty and weightless.

There was no thrill, excitement, no happiness nor happy lucky feeling like I had always imagined I would have when marrying the man I loved and with whom I would share my life.

The kiss to seal our promises occurred with no love in my heart. At that moment, I still had hope that I would have a happy life with Bijan in spite of the deep nagging of my heart.

The ceremony was over, and the party was on. All the guests were happily chatting, eating, drinking, and dancing. I looked at my sister and brother among the guests. I wanted to run to Narine and beg her to take me home, but I couldn't. I had not shared my true feelings with her. She didn't know that Bijan had scared me to death. I was as afraid of Bijan as I was of the devil himself.

Just a few hours before, I had wanted to run away, to find a safe place to hide. I didn't want to marry Bijan, but it was too late and too dangerous to share my true feelings with him now.

Even if I had the guts before the ceremony to look into his eyes and say, "I don't want to marry you." I knew there was no chance he would just say, "Okay, I can't force you." Instead, within moments, I was a married woman. I had to smile and pretend to be happy; after all, it was my wedding day.

Previously, I had asked Bijan to tell the media not to publish our wedding photos so that my parents would not see them before they returned to Tehran.

However, postponing the news was hopeless; the media was not going to stay silent. There is a saying in Farsi: "One can't ride a camel bending and hoping no one will see them." I rode the camel, and everyone could see. I had to make the best of it.

The morning after the wedding, I woke early and prepared Bijan's favorite breakfast: tea, eggs and bacon, Bulgarian cheese, fresh bread with butter and homemade jams. After placing the tray on the corner of the bed, I lay down next to him and gently kissed his cheeks, nose, and eyes. When he opened them, he pulled me into his arms and kissed me back.

"Did you sleep well Mrs. Valayati?" He asked joyfully.

"Yes, Mr. Valayati, I slept well," I responded, happily. We both laughed and joked around while having breakfast in bed. Then Bijan got ready to leave for the production studio. He kissed me and held me for a long time. Pulling me back and holding my shoulders, he looked straight into my eyes, saying, "today is the first day of your life as Mrs. Valayati, my wife. I promise I will make the happiest life for you, I will always be there for you, and I will love and cherish you. You are my wife, and I adore you." I returned his kiss and promised to be a devoted wife.

Alone, I stepped out of bed, walked into the hall, and stood looking at what was now my home. I was a married woman with a wedding ring on my finger. From now on, I would live here with my husband, Bijan.

We couldn't honeymoon, as Bijan was in the middle of his movie shoot. He was often at the studio or shooting at different sites. At home, I had nothing to do; our housekeeper did all the chores. I had no one to visit, nowhere to go. My only contacts were Narine and Edwin.

As time went on, I began to think about all I had lost; nearly everybody and everything in my former life, my family, all my friends, my relatives, my career, and most importantly, my freedom.

Bijan wasn't very social; he worked, or, when he wasn't working, he preferred, preferred to stay home. We would watch TV, play cards, or play backgammon. Bijan's two brothers, his cousin, and his few friends from the movie industry were frequent visitors.

Three weeks into our marriage, Bijan had to travel to Isfahan to finish the final scenes of his film. While he gone, I had nothing to do. I felt lonely and isolated as if I were the only soul on earth.

Twenty-five-years old and gay, our housekeeper, Ali, had become my companion and safe keeper. Bijan did not consider it a risk to have a gay man at home with me while he was away.

I could talk freely with Ali, without fear that he would report back to my husband. A very experienced cook and a great entertainer, Ali would play music and dance, filling my otherwise empty days with a bit of joy and fun.

Our home, the one Bijan had rented, was the ground floor apartment in a two-story building in northern Tehran. Surrounded by a spacious terrace and large garden, it had three bedrooms, a dining area, a living area and a receiving hall.

One room was for entertaining where Bijan had installed a screen, an eight-millimeter camera, and comfortable seats. Our bedroom had a glass door, opening to a large patio. In the corner, stairs led to a garden. Next to it was the driveway where Bijan parked his beloved car, a red Firebird.

We did not mix much with the neighbors, most of whom were very curious about how movie stars lived, but my private life was not for others' entertainment.

One ordinary morning, the telephone rang. It was Narine, sounding as if she were in a deep, remote hole. I could feel the fear in her voice.

"Linda, Dad is back." My heart sank. For a few minutes, I could not talk.

"How is he doing?" I asked hesitantly, fearing the answer.

"Terrible," Narine cried out. "He is in a horrible mood. I've never seen him this angry. He was on the verge of exploding. I wish Mom were back to comfort him. I dare not get too close. He stays in his room, crying."

Narine was crying, too. It hit me like lightening. What had I done? I would never forgive myself for the pain I had caused them.

Narine said Dad had ordered all my belongings thrown out of the house, with no reminder of me to remain, as if I had never existed. It was like cleaning a crime scene. No one could mention my name or visit me. The verdict was in: guilty. The sentence for my crime would be life in exile. To my parents, I was dead.

After hanging up, I sat for a long time. The bitter truth began to sink in. I had committed an unforgivable sin. I had known exactly how hard my wedding news would hit my parents. I should have known how they would react. It felt as if a hurricane had hit my life. Now, looking back, I could see the devastation. It was time to face the harsh reality of my action and its consequences on my family.

During my entire life, I had only seen my father cry once. It was for his brother, who had lost his sight in an accident at work. This time, my Dad's tears were for his lost child, his damaged pride, and his family's honor.

Armenian tradition required he disown me. I had brought shame and disgrace on him, and our society was going to make sure my family felt it every day of their lives.

When I shared my father's reaction with Bijan, he simply shrugged his shoulders and said, "Don't worry; they will get over it eventually." He seemed incapable of compassion for anyone but himself.

I didn't hear from Narine for ten days until she called to say that Mom was back. How I wished I could be with them again. I missed life at my parent's house, my room with posters of Che Guevara, The Bee Gees, Jimmy Hendricks and others.

I wanted to be in our kitchen, which always smelled of delicious food or in the living room filled with noise and laughter when we sat together listening to Dad's jokes and playing games.

I even missed fighting with my sisters and brother. Who could have imagined, that all these simple things would one day be out of my reach? I had lost them forever. I wondered if other girls lost this much when they got married.

Twelve

Bijan was busy with his career and movies but coveted having a child. I, on the other hand, was not at all prepared to become a mother. Before being trapped in Bijan's web, getting married and having children were at the bottom of my list. Now I was being forced to make motherhood a priority.

One evening after dinner, as Bijan and I watched a movie, a short conversation became an argument. I think it started because he had one too many drinks.

When I asked him to calm down and lower his voice, he stood up slapped me as hard as he could, then walked away to fix another drink. Furious, I started to scream at him. Not expecting my reaction, he became even more angry.

I saw his hand rising, holding his drink in a heavy crystal glass. The next moment, it was flying in my direction. All I could do was to duck and protect my head with my hands, but the glass broke against my elbow. The pain was astounding. Blood gushed from the gaping wound.

Sitting on the floor in shock and panic, I couldn't breathe, and my face was burning from the slap. There was blood all over me. I got up, walked to the bedroom, locked the door, and sat on the bed, wondering if the bone had shattered.

Uncontrollable tears rolled over my cheeks as the physical pain engulfed my entire soul. I was hurting from inside. All this time, I foolishly believed the words of love Bijan repeated often. He had promised not to hurt me anymore, especially now that I was his wife.

I took a tee-shirt out of a drawer, wrapped it around my elbow, sat on the floor, lit a cigarette, and tried to care for the wound. Within the hour, Amir, one of Bijan's brothers, arrived to take me to the emergency room. Bijan's younger brothers, Amir and Behnam were always there to clean up his messes.

At the clinic, the doctor asked, "How did this happen?"

Amir looked at me as if pleading "Please Linda, don't tell the truth."

I was not going to tell a soul how this happened. How could I admit to being a newlywed, injured by my drunken husband? I responded, "I slipped in the bathroom, and my elbow hit the glass shower door. It broke and cut me." He seemed to believe the story.

The doctor ordered a nurse to clean up the wound so he could stitch it. Hearing him, I asked for another solution. He insisted on stitches, saying that the elbow is in constant movement. Only stitches could hold the wound closed.

I begged the doctor not to use stitches, promising not to bend my arm. I think he felt sorry for me, he decided to do his best without them and made me sign off that I refused stitches against doctor's orders.

On the way back, Amir picked up pain medication prescribed by the doctor. When we arrived home, he walked me inside. The house was dark and quiet. Turning the lights on, I saw Bijan sleeping on the living room couch, next to him on the table was a half-empty bottle of whiskey.

I thanked Amir, and he left. In my empty bedroom, I sat on the edge of the bed, trying to undress with one hand, being careful not to bend my elbow. I could feel the pain deep in my bones. I took two of the pills before looking around for water.

There was none. Not wanting to pass Bijan on my way to the kitchen, I swallowed them without the water. It was easier than possibly waking him and having another confrontation.

With one hand, I slowly started to remove the bed cover. It took an eternity to undress. My arm hurt and small traces of blood seeped through the bandage. Why didn't I listen to the doctor when he said stitches were necessary? I hoped the medication would take effect and sleep would be pain-free.

But sleep would not come. The clock next to the bed said 2 a.m. I went to the window, pulled the curtain aside and stood there looking out aimlessly. It was dark out except for a pale streetlight glowing like a silver halo trying to awaken the sleeping trees.

Stepping onto the terrace, I felt the soothing crisp air and sat down, gazing into the sky. I let the tears wash my pain and sorrow away. Eventually, I went back to bed and cried myself to sleep.

Waking up at around 10:30 in the morning, I noticed a small note from Bijan pinned to my pillow. Whatever it said, it was not going to change my feelings. Without bothering to read it, I went into the living room. Huge bouquets of flowers were everywhere. The house smelled like a flower shop.

There was no sign of Bijan. He had left before I woke up. I was not impressed; the flowers only seemed as if they were covered in thorns and piercing my heart. No one had ever given me this many flowers. But neither had anyone ever caused me this much pain. All the flowers in the world couldn't take the pain away.

After one of the most painstaking baths ever, with one functional hand, I managed to change the bandage. The wound looked horrible. The gash was large and still bleeding, but not alarmingly so. Dressing was another long, but manageable process, so was breakfast. I made coffee, toasted some bread, and placed everything on a tray. But I couldn't carry it with one hand.

After a few trips, I had breakfast in bed without the usual connotations of a happy, cozy meal. An overwhelming fury began to build, taking over every inch of my body and soul. Mixed emotions erupted. I was angry, hurt, humiliated, sad, and above all else, I felt orphaned. Pain seized my elbow and crying had caused my eyes to swell. My husband had treated me worse than an animal.

What was I going to do? I didn't want to stay, yet I felt I couldn't leave. Where would I go? I couldn't return to my family after what I had done. All bridges to the past were in flames, and the path to the future with Bijan seemed dark.

I spent most of the day lying in bed, wondering what I could do. I used to love him. He had said he loved me like no other, but he hurt me. Love seemed like an empty and foreign word. After what he did, how could I feel anything but hate for him?

My frustration was not just at the pain and humiliation; it was also the strong feeling of entrapment. Why did I feel I had no place to go? Was there no one to stand up to Bijan and teach him how to be a real man and loving husband?

Bijan did not return until late that night. Already in bed, I heard the door open and the sound of his keys landing on the table near the entrance. His steps came toward the bedroom.

Taking a few steps toward the bed, he stopped, so did my heart. I pretended to be asleep, not wanting him anywhere near me; I couldn't handle it. Luckily, he turned and left the room I breathed a sign of relief, "Thank you, God."

I waited to be sure he wasn't coming back, then, sitting in my bed, I lit a cigarette. I did not want to draw Bijan's attention, so I left the light off. I felt miserably helpless, with no job, no money, no one to rescue me, and nowhere to run. If I left tomorrow, where would I end up? Despite all these reasons, I was determined to ask for a divorce.

80⚜CB

Up early, I took a shower and changed my bandage. I saw Bijan having breakfast and was caught off guard. He put down his cup, stood up, and walked toward me. I stepped back, not wanting to look at his face. He came closer, taking my good hand, saying: "Linda, I'm so sorry, believe me. I threw the glass without thinking."

He continued: "I don't know why I would hurt you like this. I love you. These two days have seemed like years. I am so sorry. Please believe me; I would never hurt you intentionally. It was a horrible accident. Please trust me. I didn't know how to approach you. I thought these flowers would show how sorry I am. Linda, I love you and I am sorry."

I pushed him away but before leaving the kitchen, turned back to look straight at his shocked face, saying firmly, "I want a divorce."

For a moment, I thought his eyes would jump out of their sockets. With disbelief in his tone, he asked: "What did you say?"

"I said I want a divorce," I snapped back.

He pulled a chair out and sat down, then took a sip of his tea, looked at me for what seemed an eternity. Waiting for his reaction, I wondered, should I be ready to duck again? Finally, he spoke. "You want a divorce? You will get it, go get ready, and let's go."

Now it was my turn to freeze in shock. Did I hear him cor-rectly? Did he say okay? Was he joking or hadn't he heard me right? Regardless, I rushed to my bedroom to change while my heart pounded at three times its normal rate. It took longer to dress with one hand. I found Bijan waiting for me in the dining room.

I looked at him and said, "I am ready to go."

Bijan looked at me and did not say anything for few minutes, then in a very calm and cold voice said: "Are you crazy? Do you think I married you to divorce you? I'm not going to divorce you, ever! Have you even thought about the media and the articles they will write about me? That our marriage didn't even last a year? Put that word out of your head."

"Why are you doing this to me?" I asked. "You said you love me and did things for me no one else has. I thought you were a knight who would take me to the land of love, but you brought me straight to hell.

"Look at my arm. Do you have any idea how much pain you've caused? Can't you see what you did? You could have killed me if my elbow didn't block my temple. You covered the house in flowers; if I stay, one day it may be my grave you cover." With no further words, I returned to the bedroom.

Iranian law denied women the right to divorce; only men had that right. I could not divorce Bijan without his approval. I didn't want to be his wife anymore. I wanted to go where he couldn't harm me. But I had nowhere to go. All I could do was have faith, to keep hope that my suffering and unbearable life with him would one day end, and I would find my way out of this mess.

Once again, I was alone with no one to help me escape. If only I could turn back time, I would never have married Bijan or left my family.

The months rushed by, and Bijan returned to being that caring and loving husband who kept me on a pedestal. He also was becoming obsessed with becoming a father. Living under his roof was a delicate game, becoming pregnant was out of the question. Despite his best behavior, I could not trust him to have changed—and his drinking continued. My only solution was to start birth control without him knowing.

Thirteen

I started taking birth control pills as Bijan waited to hear news of my pregnancy. After some months, he began to worry that we could not conceive. He likely thought that, just like his first wife, I could not become pregnant. What a lucky woman she was.

The idea of me being infertile terrified him, and he insisted on me seeing a gynecologist. I managed to avoid seeing a doctor by making excuses but eventually had to give in. The day came sooner than I had hoped.

I told the doctor I was on the pill because I was not ready to become a mother. I shared that I was having difficulty with my husband and was sure our marriage would not last.

After listening, he advised that I stop taking the pills saying, "To be so young and taking pills is not advisable, in particular, because you smoke. It is a dangerous combination. Also, taking birth control might affect your fertility. Because you have been taking the pills, your body is already immune to pregnancy for some time."

I trusted his advice and stopped taking the pills, thinking I was "immune."

My next period did not arrive. Was I pregnant? Could I not trust even my doctor?

There were only questions, no answers. I had to do something; I did not want a baby. There was no guarantee that I was going to grow old with Bijan. If I could, I would have left Bijan right then, but how could I if I was pregnant? A child would tie me to him forever; it would be like getting a life sentence.

Bijan and I continued to have sex, with him hoping to get me pregnant, not knowing I already was. Within a few days, I visited a clinic that offered early-stage terminations via injections for three consecutive days, and then I was to wait for my period to start. It was my first independent decision since getting married.

The day of the final injection, I returned home to find Bijan waiting, with a look of fury. I didn't expect him until later. Had he questioned Ali and found out where I had gone?

"Where were you?" he snapped.

He had caught me by surprise. With no time to think, I blurted that I was pregnant and had decided to terminate it. I continued, "I know how much you want to become a father, but I am not ready to become a mother."

The atmosphere was tense, but I had to go on. "I haven't the slightest idea how to take care of a newborn or be a good mother. I don't want a child, and I am sorry I can't give you one right now. I knew you wouldn't have allowed me to do what I have already done; I got injections, which will terminate the pregnancy and start my period. Now, all I have to do is to wait."

He was outraged. His whole body was shaking, he said, "How dare you make such a decision without my consent." He began to walk towards me, the one who had killed his dream. I didn't move. I was ready to face him.

When he reached me, he grabbed me by my neck, screaming "You murderer, you killed my child knowing how much I wanted one. You are a whore who just wants to sleep around. I will kill you, bitch!"

He beat me repeatedly, but I didn't feel the pain. His humiliating words didn't embarrass me. With each blow, I became more convinced I had done the right thing. Though I survived the beating, the situation at home became unbearable. Barely speaking, he spent more time away. I eagerly awaited my period. It never came. I was forced, once again, to discuss my condition with Bijan.

One night while he was watching TV, I told him that my period did not come, and I was thinking about getting an abortion out of fear the injections had already harmed the fetus. I couldn't do it without my husband's consent on paper. Otherwise, it was against the law. I explained to him that it would be better for him to sign the papers.

"Why should I?" he asked, bitterly. Staring, he added, "Don't you know how much I wanted to become a father? Now you are asking me to sign a death certificate?"

Bravely, I dared to say, "You signed it the day you raised your hand to me. Besides, after all those injections, I think it's too risky to keep the baby." I continued, "It is you who wanted a child, I didn't."

Bijan finally agreed. He had to. He signed the papers, and within two days, I had an abortion.

Unfortunately, Bijan was now aware there was nothing wrong with my fertility, taking away my chance of secretly taking the pill. He thought if I was able to bear a child, I should. He cared little for what I wanted or if I was ready for parenthood. My desires were acceptable to him only when they fit into his wishes. I desperately needed a solution.

I had never dealt with a character whose mood could change in an instant as if two people lived in one body. His drinking was a big part of the issue, as afterward, his dangerous side would emerge.

For instance, he often would say he would kill any man who looked at me or came close, despite there being no ill intention. After a bout of aggression he would become unbelievably kind, caring, gentle, and loving, sorry that he had hurt me.

Suddenly, he could not live without me. At times like these, I wanted to say to him, "How can you dare claim you love me madly?" It was only true in the psychological sense. "Mad" love destroyed whatever real love we had. Now it was killing my dreams, my soul, and my life.

Fourteen

Sorrow became my constant companion. My sister kept me informed about the family but calling just to hear their voices became a habit. When Dad would answer, my heart would beat faster, his voice reminding me of what I had gambled and lost.

I wanted to tell him how much I missed him and that I was sorry, lonely, without protection, and unloved. But it was too late to be sorry. I could only stay silent as he asked, "Hello, who's calling?"

On a depressingly cloudy day, out of misery and desperation, I dared to call my mother's cousin knowing she would likely reject me. Within a few seconds, I heard her voice with its familiar "Hello."

"Hello, Aunty, this is Linda," I said, then waited for her reaction. To my surprise, she didn't hang up, though her coldness came through the wires. "Please, Aunty, talk to my mom and convince her to see me. I miss her a lot. I need her."

"Do you realize what you are asking me to do? I wouldn't dare say a word to your mother about you," she said, angrily.

I started to cry, then begged.

"You should have thought about the consequences before you said "I do" to a Muslim," she said. "When you married a Muslim man, you knew what you were doing. You knew that it was against our Christian faith and family tradition. You disgraced your family. How can you expect your mother to be willing to see you after what you did?"

Asking for her understanding was pointless. Breaking tradition was unacceptable. But how could tradition be more important than one's child? As if feeling my pain, she showed some compassion. "It might be a good idea to visit our Armenian Church on Sundays," she said. "You know your mother attends. When was the last time you went?"

Caught off guard, I said, "Not since I got married."

She replied, "Well, after what you've done, may God have mercy on you," and hung up the phone.

৪০৯৯৫৫৪৩

Bijan had just returned from a month-long work trip. Behaving with kindness and care, he expressed how much he had missed me. He began to spend more time at home, saying it held whatever he wanted, and I was the woman of his dreams.

We went out more often, and I grew content that we were happy, without his usual outbursts. However, in the back of my mind, I knew something was not right.

Within a week of his return, I started to have feminine itching and burning. I did not know what was happening. Each time I used the bathroom or had sex, the sensation would almost kill me. It was intolerable. Bijan suggested I go to the doctor.

I called the same gynecologist who had told me my body was immune to pregnancy, wondering what he would say this time? I got a same-day emergency appointment. With Bijan at work, I took a cab through the terrible traffic of Tehran, praying to God for help. The ride to the doctor seemed to take forever.

Upon arriving, I paid the driver and rushed into the building, forgoing the elevator, I ran up the stairs. Entering that crowded waiting room, I went straight to the receptionist, telling her it was an extreme emergency. Smiling politely, she said, "There are few other emergencies before yours."

I wanted to slap her; the itching and burning were making me irritable. With no choice, I found a seat, picked up a magazine, and waited uncomfortably for thirty long minutes. Finally, she called my name, and I rushed into the doctor's office. The doctor greeted me with a big smile, saying "How nice to see you Ms. Linda, have a seat."

"Doctor, please help me, I don't know what kind of a disease it is, but for a few days, I have had horrible burning and itching. It is killing me. I can't sleep, walk, or sit." He frowned, saying, "Let's see what is going on." Pointing to the exam table, he told me to change and lie down.

I was feeling self-conscious and tense when he came in, gloves on, to examine me. Noticing my obvious discomfort, he said, "Relax, this won't take long."

Afterward, I got dressed as fast as I could in anticipation of what he found. Sitting behind his desk writing on a pad, he finally raised his head and sternly said, "You have a sexually transmitted disease, I am going to . . ."

I didn't understand. He was talking nonsense. "That's impossible. I only have sex with my husband. How could I . . ." Before I could finish, reality hit me like lightning. I got this dreadful virus from Bijan, my husband. Just as quickly, a second bolt struck. He is cheating on me. "You low-life son of a bitch," I muttered to myself.

I thought about his recent behavior. The bastard was acting kind and loving, knowing he was screwing diseased women, then bringing an STD home to me. How low could he go? Burning with anger and disappointment, I wondered how Bijan could shamelessly play the role of the Romeo after having done this. He had opened yet another bitter reality in my life. Thoughts raced as if he had slapped me once again.

Broken and humiliated, I began to talk to the doctor. "I didn't know what was wrong. I did not expect to be infected by my husband. It was devastating.

"He's betrayed me, screwed around, and brought a disease back to me," I said to the doctor, not mentioning the beatings and violent behavior. Tears started to roll. The image of Bijan in bed with another would not leave my mind.

In a soothing voice, the doctor said, "You know, this doesn't surprise me. I see wives like you every day. Unfortunately, this has become part of life, but you should be strong. Men are weak when it comes to sex. Your husband is an actor, exposed to hundreds of women every day. It is harder for him to fight the temptation."

Looking at him in disbelief, angrily I said, "Are you serious, doctor? Are you trying to calm me down? Your explanation makes me sick to my stomach. No thanks for the 'comforting' words about how men succumb to temptation, married or not."

I stood up, took the prescription, and walked toward the door, hoping this was the last time I would see him. Before leaving, I heard him say, "Don't forget to tell your husband to come and see me. He needs medication, too."

ಹಾ⚘ಂ

Stepping out of the building, I stood still, not ready to go home. I needed to gather myself. Behind large, dark sunglasses, I wandered aimlessly through the streets of Tehran. In just the last few hours, I had grown very, very old. Marrying Bijan had cost a lot. I had lost everything and gained nothing at all. The reality of carrying an STD terrified and worried me. How could my husband have done this to me? It was like a declaration of war. I had lost respect for him long ago, but he meant nothing to me after this. Infidelity was the last straw.

I was even angrier at myself. My cowardly behavior had brought me this low. What had happened to the proud and confident Linda? Was she alive or dead? When was the moment of death? A date came to my mind, the day of her wedding. That day had also been the day of her funeral. That is what happened to her.

I don't remember how long I had been walking, but it was getting dark. I entered a corner drug store to get my medication and then hailed a cab to head home. It struck me that it would never again be home to me. It was more like a torture chamber.

In the cab, I rehearsed what I would say to my cheating husband. I was carrying the painful proof of his unfaithfulness. The driver, a tired-looking old man, smiled contently while looking at me in the mirror. It made me uncomfortable.

When he noticed I was annoyed, he said, "Sorry, Ma'am, but I am so happy to be your driver. It is rare to have a movie actress in my cab. My family and I have seen all your movies. We all love you, so much, but you stopped acting." He paused, then said, "May I ask you a question?"

I was not expecting to be recognized. It made me uncomfortable, considering the situation.

"It depends on the question," I replied. He had more than one.

"Excuse me, I don't want to be rude or nosy, but why did you marry Bijan Valayati? What a waste. I remember your first movie. I took my whole family to see it, after that we went to see all of your films. My children still have your posters on their walls. Are you going to play in the movies again? Could I have your autograph for my kids?"

I thanked him for his kind words, signed an autograph, but did not answer his questions. I had no answers. He declined to charge the fare, repeating it had been an honor to have me as a passenger. I thanked him and I gave him a very large tip instead. At his age, he should have been enjoying life instead of still working to provide for his family.

ॐ

Standing at the door, I heard the keys rattling in my hands as they began to shake. I felt sick to my stomach. Inside, I put the bag of medication on the table and went to my bedroom. The sound of running water coming from the bathroom meant Bijan was taking a shower; perhaps trying in vain to clean his dirty body.

A few minutes later, a towel around his waist, he entered the bedroom. When he saw me sitting on the edge of the bed, his expression changed. "What is wrong honey? You look as if you are returning from a funeral."

"Yes, I am. I just buried our marriage." He seemed puzzled about what I was saying. He was either slow or pretending to know nothing.

"I am back from my gynecologist," I replied. Still confused, his face lit up. "Are you pregnant? Are you carrying my baby? Why are you so grief stricken?" he asked with anticipation.

"No, I am not carrying your baby. I'm carrying your STD." My voice broke. Talking was becoming more difficult. Bijan said nothing. "Since our marriage started, I've taken all your crap, every beating, every humiliation. I have put up with you, but this is beyond tolerance. It is unforgivable. I can't even look at you; I am ashamed of being your wife."

He stepped toward me, as I raised my hand motioning him not to come any closer.

He sat on the floor, looked at me, and began to talk. "You are my love and my life. You are the best thing that has ever happened to me. Why would I betray you? Why would I hold another woman's body in my arms? How could you even think I am capable of going so low?" He continued with tears in his eyes.

"I have not been feeling well myself. As an actor, I have love scenes. One might get an STD even from a kiss. How could I have known if they were sick and could infect me, too? They could have the slightest open wound in their mouth, and then through the saliva, the virus could transfer. Please, Linda, do some research. Educate yourself; then you can accuse me of being unfaithful."

How calm and self-assured he was as he planted seeds of doubt. Was it saliva or semen? The disease was "sexually trans-mitted." Does he know more than my doctor? Impossible.

His last words were, "You know how much I love you. I don't need any other woman." These words sounded familiar. Years before, I had heard the same bullshit.

After a week on medication, my body returned to normal. I was physically cured, but not emotionally. Despite trying to believe Bijan, I came back to doubt. I could no longer trust him. "Was my husband unfaithful?" I would wonder. "Of course, you idiot," would be my reply.

Fifteen

Weeks later, I rallied my strength and courage for a Sunday morning visit to the Armenian Church in hopes of seeing my mother or at least finding solace from my miserable life.

On the way, prayers that no one would recognize me filled my mind. I feared they would point and say, "That is the woman who married a Muslim." I altered my appearance in anticipation of such embarrassment.

This had been my family's Church since my early childhood. My affection for it and my Christian faith had grown across many events, from regular services to weddings, baptisms, Easter services and even funerals. On this Sunday, I had come desperately seeking the comfort of the Holy Spirit.

As one of the few Armenian churches in Tehran, it was always crowded. Today was no exception, and I could not find my mother in the crowd.

Across the weeks, I left each service not having seen my mother. Perhaps God, too, was punishing me.

As my twenty-second birthday approached, I spent an evening contemplating that it would be my first birthday as a married woman and would be without my family to celebrate with me.

Bijan wasn't home. He had gone to the studio to reshoot some scenes. I watched TV, had dinner, went into my bedroom with a book, and laid there feeling depressed and forgotten.

Over the radio, Wolfman Jack, the famous American D.J., cheered me up with songs that seemed to caress and soothe my soul. I tried to relax, when suddenly "Knights in White Satin" came on. Bernard and I had danced and kissed to that song. It was "our" song.

I wondered what he was doing. Who was he kissing now? I turned off the radio, overwhelmed with emotion from all that had happened since those innocent dances.

Bijan's voice woke me. "Why are you sleeping so early, honey?" He was standing next to the bed, touching my face. Puzzled and still sleepy, I looked at the clock. "Bijan, it is two o'clock in the morning, why did you wake me up?"

He smelled of alcohol. Not answering, he undressed, scattering his clothes across the floor, and threw himself on the bed. In a few minutes, he had passed out, snoring. I studied him while he slept. Here was my husband and partner, the one who should be there to love, support, and protect me throughout my life.

The smell of alcohol became unbearable and was making me sick. I went to the kitchen and sat there thinking about our life together. It occurred to me he could not have been returning from the studio in that condition. Where had he spent the evening?

I thought he had wanted to marry me but wondered why, when as a famous and handsome ladies' man, he could have remained single and had any woman he wanted.

Why did he choose me? The more I thought, I could see we didn't have a single thing in common; whatever he liked, I disliked; whatever I approved of, he would dismiss. Finding even one similar interest was difficult.

The next Sunday, I went to church hoping God had some special gift in store. I went straight to a little chapel in the corner of the main hall decorated with portraits of Jesus, Mary, and many saints.

People gathered there to light candles and pray before joining the mass. The glow of the candles created a holy tranquility in the room, as well as with the parishioners, who each seemed to suffer some physical, emotional or spiritual pain. Together, we all sought healing.

I lit six candles, one for each member of my family and one for myself, then knelt in front of a portrait of Mary, the holy mother, and began to pray. My soul needed healing, and my body needed comfort.

I begged God to forgive me and grant the miracle of returning everything I had once. My body and soul were broken. Only my parents' love could mend them. Drowning in my spiritual quest, I felt a hand touch my shoulder.

Turning to see if perhaps some frail woman might be leaning on me for help getting up, or worse, that someone may have recognized me, my eyes opened as I turned around. I found myself staring straight into the tear-filled eyes of my mother.

Not believing what I saw, I closed my eyes again. It had to be my imagination, I thought, an illusion, a sweet dream. I kept my eyes shut, trying to hold onto the image, as my mother's soothing voice said, "Open your eyes, Linda; look at me, it's your mother."

Slowly I turned, still not daring to open my eyes. I felt the warmth of her body as she came close, opening her arms to embrace me. Thank you, dear God. It was real. I let myself drown in her love, holding her tightly, smelling her familiar scent, while kissing her soft cheeks. Now crying, I asked for forgiveness, "Mama, I am so, so sorry. Please forgive me."

We left the church still holding hands. I clutched her hand as if to prevent losing her again. She agreed to extend our visit at a coffee shop but mentioned she should be home before noon.

We found a quiet spot. Once settled at our table, the words began tumbling out of my mouth in a rush, like machine gun fire.

"Mama, you don't know how important it is for me to see you. I know what I did was wrong; I should not have married Bijan. I can't change things now, but I am asking for your forgiveness. I can't live without my family. You can't imagine how lonely my life is. I am sad and suffering without you and the rest of my family."

The waiter interrupted as he set our coffees on the table. When he left, I asked, "Mom, how is Dad?" Her eyes, once again, filled with tears. After being quiet for a time, she looked straight into my eyes, said, "He's not well. He is no longer talkative and spends most of his time in his study. When he comes out, you can tell he has been crying.

"It has been like this since he saw your wedding photos in the newspaper. Of course, at home, he does not speak of you. Nobody dares to, but a few times, I have seen your photo on his desk."

Still crying, she couldn't continue. I took her hand, but she would not be comforted.

After a while, she dried her eyes and asked, "Tell me about your life, how is it?" I lied. "It's okay mom. Everything is alright." To change the subject, I asked, "Mom, can I see you again?"

She smiled and agreed, saying, "I have missed you enormously since I returned from Armenia. Nothing is the same at home. Your dad misses you too, but pretends you are no longer his daughter."

When it was time to part, I panicked. "Mama, don't go please," I begged. "Stay a bit longer." I wanted to look at her face, hold her hands, and stay in her sheltering arms.

"Child, you should have thought about this earlier," she replied. "No one forced you to marry him. You did it regardless of the horrendous consequences. From our point of view, you sold us out for a man with a bad reputation who isn't even part of our faith. You made your choice. Now, stop crying."

Her comforting hands reached out with a tissue to wipe the tears and pain from my face, as they had throughout my life. God only knew how I had missed those hands.

Later at home, I could hardly wait for Bijan's return. Getting to see my mother and being in her arms had been like Christmas all over again.

Finally, he arrived, and I didn't spare a minute before telling him all about it. Equally excited, he held me in his arms, saying soon I would be able to see my whole family.

Before letting go, he kissed me tenderly and added, "I am so happy to see the sparks of happiness in your eyes again. I love you so much and don't want to see you sad."

Life seemed to be gradually changing for the better. Bijan was being kind and had stopped lashing out. Now the highlight was seeing my mother again. My tormented soul and body was beginning to heal. I felt alive for the first time in a long while, then came the best birthday present ever.

༺ ༜ ༻

In the spring of 1975, we traveled with friends to the Caspian Sea for a week's vacation at a huge villa during perfect weather. Each morning, on the terrace facing the sea, we sat for breakfast, breathing the sea air, as the calm breeze caressed our bodies and souls. Delicious fresh fish, rice with saffron, and local herbs made eating seem like a fiesta in heaven. It was the peaceful vacation for which I had hoped.

The calm would not last the summer. My period late and feeling queasy, I took a pregnancy test. It came back positive, once again. Hearing the news, Bijan cried tears of joy, held me tightly, and kissed me tenderly.

I was happy for him but not for myself. Twenty-two years of age seemed too young to become a mother. I still was not ready, but another abortion seemed worse than having a child.

I was to meet my mother in a couple of weeks at her cousin's house. How was I going to tell her the news? I feared telling her would cause her to cut me off again and leave forever. It would be her first grandchild, but also, a half Muslim one.

The entire week had me thinking about how to break the news to her. What should I say first? How would she react? My head was spinning, with no idea of the outcome. It was not like I could hide it for long.

Just three days before seeing my mom, Bijan and I argued. I had gone out without letting him know. He was fuming, eyes red with fury and drunk again.

At the dinner table, he asked, "Don't you know I demand to know every step you take? You act like a teenager, doing whatever you please. You are a married woman. Why would you go out wearing jeans?" He wasn't making sense. I didn't understand why he was upset about my wearing jeans.

I answered: "Nonsense! Since when are jeans not for married women? I went window shopping for cute baby clothes. I didn't realize I needed your permission. What is wrong with what I did, and why should I report my every step? You leave me alone here for weeks. How is that right? Now I go out for a few hours, and you make a scene? I'm tired of explaining myself. Maybe you should eat alone."

I stood up to leave when a dish came flying toward me. Bijan stood up, kicked his chair away, and walked over. Grabbing my hair, he threw me to the floor and began punching me. "You whore. I'll teach you to obey. I am going to show you who is the boss in this house."

The beating continued without regard for the child I was carrying. Fighting back and trying to free myself, I shouted: "You're crazy! You sick son of a bitch. Do you think I'm your slave? I hate you, you animal, I'm tired of pretending everything's okay. Tomorrow I'll call the newspapers and tell them what an animal you are."

I immediately regretted the threat. His anger and aggression got worse. While kicking, punching, and slapping me, he said, "Okay, then let me give you something to tell your boyfriend reporters."

Against his strength, all I could do was protect my belly, the rest of my body was exposed. Then the phone rang, and he stopped. After a few more rings he let go of me and went to answer it. After speaking briefly, he hung up.

I was frozen in terror, waiting for him to finish the job. Instead, he went to the bedroom, changed clothes, and left the house, without even looking to see if I was alive or his baby was alright.

Minutes later, I heard his car engine fading slowly into the distance. That caller had saved my unborn child and me. Alone, I thanked whoever it might have been on the phone.

Movement was painful. I couldn't stand without falling. Clothes torn, the taste of blood in my mouth, I managed to crawl to the bathroom, reach to fill the tub and roll into it. The mirror showed a cut on my lip and a bloody nose. Bruises covered me, head to toe.

The soothing water ran over my belly. My thoughts were of my baby. How was he or she doing? Did the baby feel what we went through? Was the baby hurt? The thought brought tears to my eyes. What would be the destiny of this innocent child? Could the baby survive having a monster for a father? Briefly, abortion entered my mind. Maybe it would be better for this child than a life of misery.

Suddenly, I came to my senses. How could I give my baby a choice to live or die? I was doing to the child what my husband had been doing to me. Right then, I vowed to protect my baby from all harm, yet not knowing how. Was I capable? Could I even protect myself?

But in the back of my mind, I felt the baby was pulling me deeper into the trap my husband was trying to keep me in. Contradicting thoughts tortured me. Was I happy or unhappy to be pregnant? Was I hopeful or losing my faith? Happiness seemed beyond reach. Life with Bijan was like walking a tight-rope with no safety net; at any moment I could fall to my death.

Sixteen

Finally, I was on my way to see my mother at her cousin's. Luckily, I was able to hide my still bruised body under my clothes. I contemplated telling her how horribly Bijan was treating me and that I was pregnant.

I wouldn't be able to hide it much longer. But I felt as if telling my mother the truth would only hurt her more deeply. I had already caused her more than enough pain.

I arrived first, which gave me time to talk with my mom's cousin, thinking she could help. But I soon changed my mind. Still confused and scared, I couldn't do it. The anticipation of Mom's reaction was heart stopping.

Fifteen minutes later, Mom arrived. Heart pounding, I threw myself into her arms, holding her tight, not wanting to let go. After a while she said, "Linda, you are suffocating me, relax." She pulled back, caressing my cheek and smiling. A question came to her expression. As if seeing me for the first time, she looked directly into my eyes and asked, "Are you pregnant, Linda?"

I froze. How did she know? It was not physically apparent yet. Still, a weight had been lifted. Days of inner debate were in vain. I asked, "How did you know?" She sat down, motioning me to sit as well.

"I knew sooner or later this would happen," she said. "When a woman gets pregnant, she radiates a certain glow.

Something subtle changes that is hard to explain. Today, I saw that glow from you."

She wasn't angry. Rather, she seemed to have surrendered to what life had thrown at her. Of course, she wasn't jumping up and down with excitement at becoming a grandmother either, but I had not expected the calmness.

Perhaps she found it bittersweet. She was going to have her first grandchild, after all. But her traditions would prefer a Christian father. Concerned, she began to ask about my pregnancy, if I had morning sickness and other things about having a baby. I assured her that I was fine.

I felt relieved she didn't ask about life with Bijan. The truth would have been humiliating. I was married to a monster in the body of a man. Explaining to my mother that my husband had raised his hands to beat her pregnant daughter would remain a secret.

Before parting, I told my mother that I yearned to see my family and former home. Of course, this was something she already knew. It was a theme each time we met. "Mama, you can't imagine how much I've missed Dad. Please talk to him and ask his forgiveness. Tell him I am dying to see him. Please, Mom, I want to see him."

"Be patient, and I will see what I can do, no promises, though. You know very well this isn't an easy subject to discuss with him."

80❀03

I had the feeling that mom would never get around to talking to Dad about me, especially now that I was pregnant. It would not be easy for her. I again wished I had not married.

Marrying Bijan had totally changed my life, a change so drastic that I couldn't adapt. I had become an unhappy pregnant woman, instead of the happy young girl I had been. It simply was not part of my life's dreams and seemed so foreign to me, like I was on the wrong planet.

Days turned into weeks, and weeks into months, still no change at home or news from my mother regarding any conversation with my father.

My growing belly made it obvious I was pregnant. Narine and Edwin would visit me from time to time, of course without letting Dad know. During one such visit, Edwin informed me he had passed his English proficiency exam and some other required tests and was leaving Iran for England in two months. He had enrolled in college there. Dad would support him financially until his return after graduation.

The news saddened me at first because I would not see him for such a long time, but I was happy for him. It was an achievement to study in Europe. I recalled my similar opportunity, but I had turned it down. Edwin was to leave before my child was due. I promised to send photos.

A few days later Narine called, "Linda, Mom says that you should come for lunch this coming Friday."

"What?" I asked in disbelief. Narine could hear my imminent heart attack.

"I know this is going to be difficult for all of us, especially for Dad and you, but just think about being home again. Isn't that what you wanted all this time?"

"Yes," I mumbled. She was right. When we hung up, I sat next to the phone in shock. Despite it being long-overdue good news, the thought of looking at my father after all this time, vividly remembering what I had done to them, broke my heart. I started to sob uncontrollably.

I had broken my family's heart and above that, the family's honor and pride. I wondered if Bijan had turned out to be the husband I had wished for if I still would have felt so guilty about my family. My husband's wild and unkind behavior had pushed me further into the well of guilt.

It was Tuesday; I wondered how I would survive three days of anxiety, self-judgment, and mental torment. The hours might swallow me. How would I be able to sleep? Mainly, I was joyful. Finally, I could go home to be with my family. I could visit my past and all the things I had left behind. I could go to my room, which would be like heaven.

Bijan got home around seven. He had just started a new movie and was tired, but excited and in a good mood. At the dinner table, he spoke nonstop about the plot, his character, and the crew. Of course, I knew them all. I used to work with them too. But that didn't matter right now. My mind was busy thinking about Friday.

"Narine called and said I am invited for lunch at my parents' on Friday. They've forgiven me."

Bijan grinned, saying, "Didn't I tell you they would get over it? Parents forgive their children, no matter what. Plus, you didn't do anything wrong; you just married a man who isn't Armenian. I don't understand what you mean by 'be forgiven.' I don't see a sin here."

"For heaven's sake," I said. "You should be the first to understand. Your family was against our marriage, too. Your mother didn't attend our wedding because I'm not a Muslim. Do you understand their point of view now?"

He had nothing to say.

All that mattered was that I would be facing my father - in my fifth month of pregnancy. Lying in bed later that night, I began to share my deep feelings with Bijan.

"Although I'm excited about Friday, I feel scared to face them," I said. "I don't know what to say or how to act. How am I going to look into my father's eyes, knowing my actions caused him so much anguish? It is like telling him 'Yes, Dad, I knew what I was doing, but I did it anyway,' or 'Dad, I had to do it, I had no choice.'"

I realized I had said too much. I expected Bijan to ask in anger, "What do you mean by saying you had no other choice?" I looked for his reaction, but he had dozed off into a deep sleep. My entire body sighed in relieve. He had not heard a word I said.

Seventeen

Early Friday, I snuck out of bed to have a cup of tea in peace before facing the big day. Again, sheer pleasure and pure panic took over. I was grateful I could go home, yet anxious about the conversation I was going to have with my father about my dishonoring them.

We'd all had to pay or my mistake of defying tradition. I did not follow the family path, and in breaking the rules, I caused a scandal. It seemed people would never forget what I had done.

Sitting in the living room relaxing, I caressed my unborn baby through my tummy and thought about the need to consider its wellbeing. Also on my mind was the stress of this day, both good and bad, and the ongoing stress of life with Bijan. Little did I know just how much more my baby and I were to go through together.

Meanwhile, Bijan saw me on his way to the bathroom and joined me on the couch, hugging and kissing me, while patting my belly, saying, "You are awake early. I bet you didn't sleep last night."

"I'm too nervous about everything and can't sleep, can't eat, can't walk, can't talk, can't even breathe."

He started to kiss me again, hugging me tightly, saying, "Everything will be alright, believe me, I can't wait to see your happy face when you get back." Then he added, "By the way, aren't I invited?"

A moment of sheer dread came over me. Then, without waiting for my response, he said, "Just kidding! I know this is between you and your family. I understand that, sweetheart."

That was incredible. He could be so supportive and understanding, very gentle and kind, one minute, yet when angry, drunk, or both, he would become a completely different person, a mean and vicious creature.

Arriving at my parents' place around noon, I climbed the stairs like a ten-year-old, and in only a few seconds I was standing at the front door. My knees started to shake. What was about to happen? Shame and guilt overwhelmed me. How could I look into my father's eyes?

All through my childhood, intentionally disappointing my Dad, hurting his pride, or breaking his heart would never have entered my mind. But that is just what I had been doing, and grievously, making my family the target of mass judgment.

They had also suffered abandonment by relatives and friends, which had destroyed my father's pride. They blamed him for not being able to stop his daughter from breaking one of the most honored Armenian traditions.

I don't know how long I had been standing there before gathering the courage to ring the bell. Its sound echoed inside, and the door swung open. It was Anais, my little sister. She jumped into my arms and started kissing me. I cried with joy.

As we stood clinging to each other, she suddenly asked, "Why are you traveling so much? I don't see you anymore. I miss you. I don't like it when you are gone."

For a moment, her question confused me. Then I realized the family had kept the truth from her. She did not know I was married and had left home. Why should they tell her? She was too young to grasp the situation. I promised Anais to not travel for so long again, still holding her in my arms, I started toward the kitchen.

Being home again brought such joy. The bright hallway with pretty plants in a corner and the smell of my mom's delicious food were all with me once again. There was my mother, I hugged her and kissed her soft cheeks. She seemed happy and relaxed. I asked, "Mama, where is the rest of the family?"

She dried her hands, kissed me several times, and, holding my hand in hers, walked me into the dining room where Narine and Edwin were setting the table. Both smiled and jumped in my direction.

The three of us were holding each other, cheering when Anais joyously shouted: "Linda promised not to travel anymore." We all laughed at her innocent outburst.

I told Narine I was dying to go to our room. Voice lowered, she whispered, "First, you should see Dad." Of course; I knew that. Being home and with my family again gave me strength to face one of the most difficult situations of my life...sitting in front of my father, looking into his eyes and explaining why I had done what I had.

I kissed my sister and brother, saying, "It's hard to face Dad." Narine squeezed my hand, trying to comfort me. "Don't worry," she said. "Dad is glad to see you. He's been happy for a few days now."

Together again and within the safety of my family, I looked at Mom and asked where Dad was. She motioned toward the study. A shiver went through my body, but I knew it was time to face him. Mom hugged me, as if to give me courage then said, "Go on. Say hello to your father. He is waiting for you."

My legs were out of sync as I walked to his study, one wanting to run, the other was hardly moving forward. My soul was in a hurry to see him, but my body was not cooperating. Finally, there I was. Behind that door, the dearest person in my world was waiting. Cautiously, I knocked.

"Come on in," I heard and entered. There he was, in an armchair, looking tired. I stood looking at him. He stood up, after few moments I managed to step forward, trying not to cry. Burying myself in his arms, I could hold my tears no longer. I was in the place that always gave me comfort, support, and unconditional love, my father's arms.

We were both crying. Him for his lost daughter, me for my lost family. I stayed in his arms, crying and trying to talk.

"Papa, I'm sorry, please forgive me for breaking your heart and our tradition and causing so much humiliation and pain for you and my family. None of you deserved it. I will never forgive myself for what I have done. I need my family. I am so unhappy and miserable, so lonely and lost without you and your love."

I didn't tell him about my misery and painful life with Bijan or how my biggest wish was to turn back time to when I was not yet married.

Dad pulled back and started to dry my tears. I sat next to him holding his old and tired hands in my sad ones, as he said, "What's happened, has happened.

"I was against your marriage, not only because of traditions and beliefs but for your own good. My tears were mainly for you and your life, then for my humiliation. I always believed Bijan was not worthy of you. You chose to marry him anyway. I can only hope my judgment of his character was wrong."

He was hurt. I could hear the pain in his voice. It had lost its natural joyfulness, and his beautiful honey colored eyes looked sad. His hair was much grayer. What had I done? I had caused him to lose his pride. I wondered, "Will I ever be able to forgive myself?"

I loved them, but I had hurt them, exactly what my husband was doing to me. Why do we hurt those we love? How can love and pain coexist? It doesn't seem possible. I sat there, overwhelmed with guilt.

Just then, Mom came in, followed by my siblings. Looking very fondly at my father, she put her hand on his shoulder, saying, "Lunch is ready, and we're starving. Let's eat."

It seemed as if nothing had changed. It felt like I had never left and was still single. Just like the good old days around the table, and despite Dad's usual rule of not talking while eating, we all were happily chatting. During lunch, I noticed my father and mother watching me then looking at each other with questioning eyes.

When it came time to leave, I did not want to take one step out of that house. Everything I loved was there including my safety. However, I could not do what I pleased. That had brought me to this point, and now I had to go home to my husband, the father of my child.

On my way home in the car as each second took me further from them, I started to wonder once again, why did all this have to happen? My life had changed so drastically. Why was my sin so unforgivable that I had to pay such a high price? Was this a punishment from God? Why? I had not intentionally harmed anyone.

I had enough of such thoughts. What mattered was having my family back and being able to visit them. Having already inflicted so much pain, I was not going to tell them of my marital problems, especially now that I was pregnant. Sharing my misery would only lead to more suffering for them. I had to go through it alone.

Eighteen

My days swung between boredom and tension. At eight months, I was getting heavier by the day and unable to visit friends without Bijan's approval. The few people we socialized with were his friends. If I wanted to spare his wrath, it was a constant game of caution, detecting his fluctuating moods and acting accordingly.

Then we got an invitation to the first Iranian International Film Festival. Bijan said we could go. The news was my first joy since seeing my family. Finally, we would socialize as a couple within the familiar and exciting world of the movie scene. After so much seclusion, I could hardly imagine how much fun it would be.

I got to shop for an evening gown, choosing a beautiful pale blue Chanel, simple yet elegant. I spent the afternoon primping. First, my hair stylist came to style my hair, keeping it long, straight, and loose around my shoulders. I did my own makeup; I was good at it. While dressing, I looked in the mirror. A beaming 8-month-pregnant woman's glowing face looked back at me. I liked what I was seeing.

Bijan was in the salon waiting for me, looking very handsome in an elegant European-tailored dark suit and gorgeous white shirt, with a matching silk tie. Stepping into the hall, I asked, "How do I look?"

He put down the newspaper, stared at me for a long time, and then said: "We are not going."

I couldn't believe what I was hearing. I asked in disbelief, "What did you say?"

"I said we are not going," he replied sharply. Then he stood, went to the bedroom, changed into jeans and sweatshirt, came back, picked up his newspaper, and completely ignored me. I had been standing there, motionless, the entire time. Seeing that he had changed his outfit meant he was serious. We were not going.

I could not control my anger, despite the risk. "Why you are doing this? Why are we not going?" What the hell is wrong with you?"

He did not answer. There could be only one reason. His morbid jealousy was ruining everything. Even my swollen belly couldn't give him confidence that men wouldn't look at me. Besides, who would make a pass at a woman about to give birth?

I'd had enough of this game and his madness. This was a big event. My anticipation had been building for so long. I was not going to let him destroy it. I had made up my mind that I would go alone – or at least attempt it.

"You might not want to go, but I am going. Either you go with me, or I am going to call a cab and go alone. I picked up the phone.

Bijan shouted: "You had better not dare to take a step out of this house."

"I am going to show you how I dare. I am sick and tired of dancing to your tune. Tonight, I dance to my tune." Ignoring, his threat, I walked to the door. Before so much as a step outside, I felt him grab my hair, pull me back inside and slam the door.

Face to face, our eyes met: his furious. He was ready to tear me apart. His hand landed on my face, slapping me right and left. Meanwhile, he was shouting something about me only wanting to go so I could flirt and show off.

"With my big belly?" I shouted back. Beautiful, eligible women would fill the room. No one was looking forward to pregnant ones. He just could not grasp that I was his wife and had been looking forward to us proudly entering the huge ballroom together.

He seemed oblivious to my condition, still clutching my hair. He pushed me towards the bedroom. I tried to free myself, but it was no use. I could never compete with him physically. He was even stronger when adrenalin was fueling his wild state.

"You crazy bastard," I yelled, "You're psycho." I wasn't finished telling him off when he pulled my hair backward. He pushed me towards the bed. When I fell on it, a clump of hair remained in his hand. Seeing it, I moved my hands toward my scalp, where a bald spot the size of quarter burned at the top of my head.

I stood, glared at him in hate and rushed toward the door. He grabbed me. Then a kick landed on my stomach. I was in shock as I tried to support my baby. Bijan finally left, cursing. Nose bleeding, scalp burning, I was under extreme stress over the possibility of giving birth early - or even worse, that the baby, and I would both die at the hands of Bijan that night. I said a prayer that God would keep the baby safe.

Bijan slept in the living room. Unable to sleep, I sat on my bed, holding my stomach and constantly checking for bleeding. My child had not moved since the kick to my belly. I began to talk to my belly, "Don't worry, baby, mommy is here. She will take care of you. Just try to be strong; wait a little bit.

When you are born, we can run away, so your father won't find us. Just be patient, and please, please, please be okay."

I hated Bijan more than ever. He had destroyed everything. Although he repeatedly said he would be the best husband and would make me the happiest woman, my experience of being his wife was far from a happy one.

I had been a carefree girl when I married him. Now, nothing was left of me. All I wanted was for God to save my child. I was afraid to fall sleep, not knowing if the baby was okay. I had to stay awake in case I started bleeding. The night passed with no bleeding. Fortunately, we both survived the brutal attack.

&)⚜(രൂ

One morning in January of 1976, shortly after waking, I walked toward the hall. The first step brought a strange sound from within, as if something snapped, then water began to run down my leg. Not being familiar with water breaking, I was horrified, having no idea what was happening.

I called out to Bijan. As soon as he saw me, he ran to call the doctor who told him to take me to the hospital. Meanwhile, my Dad had called, wanting me to have lunch with the family, but Bijan told them we were on our way to the hospital.

In a great panic, Bijan drove wildly through the early morning snow covered streets of Tehran. At eight-thirty, I was admitted, and at a quarter past two, I gave birth by caesarean section.

Somewhere between consciousness and unconsciousness, I could see blurred faces around my bed. Bijan had gathered family and some friends. I could distinguish my mother's face, as she stood next to the bed, and my sister Anais, with a curious look.

Smiling, I motioned for her to come close, kissed her cheek, and said, "You are an auntie now!" Then it occurred to me that I did not know the gender of my child. I turned to the crowd and asked if it was a boy or a girl. "It's a boy," someone said.

I looked at Anais and said, "Let's see your nephew; I haven't seen him myself yet." The nurse brought him and placed him in my arms, whispering that I should feed him and then she politely asked everyone to leave.

There he was. Our first encounter face-to-face, we finally met. I held the little stranger in my arms, checking every inch of him in amazement. His cute little feet, tiny hands, long fingers and shining gorgeous brown eyes were all perfect.

"Hi baby, it's me, your mother... after nine months we finally see each other. You have so much hair on your head little boy, and the most beautiful and gorgeous big dark brown eyes, with the longest lashes I have ever seen. Do you know how long I have been waiting to hold and welcome you to the world and into my life? Nine long months, honey."

It was an amazing feeling, having this beautiful being in my arms and close to my heart, one whom, just a few hours ago, I didn't know. He smelled like sweet biscuit. With his long fingers, I thought he might be a piano player.

Bijan had arranged a suite at the hospital for the baby and me, but still, it felt crowded. My in-laws just had their first male grandchild. It seemed the whole dynasty was at the hospital. They all wanted to see the boy.

But my mind was consumed with planning our escape. The real joy of becoming a mother eluded me. I felt having the baby reduced my chances of getting away. With a million reasons to love my child, there was one not to: his birth lessened my chance of freedom.

During my week in the hospital, I cried every evening. When asked why I was crying, I would blame sunset for making me melancholy. Upon leaving the hospital, panic ensued. I had no idea how to care for a newborn. How would I manage? What would I do?

Nineteen

During the first few days at home, doubts and questions plagued my mind. When I was changing, bathing, or feeding the baby, I was confused. Do I love this baby? Was he going to stop me from leaving my husband? What should I do with him? Running away alone seemed much easier. I wondered if these feelings were normal. They made me feel guilty. I shared them with no one.

I had barely adjusted to married life, never mind mother-hood. It seemed I had no time to grow and mature before gaining the life experience to choose motherhood and be successful at it.

I knew becoming a mother was meant to be a rewarding and precious thing, but Bijan had turned it into a bitter and insecure exercise. The c-section incision was healing, contrary to the wound in my soul, which deepened with passing time.

It took me some months to adjust, but soon I had fallen in love with the baby, whom I named James, and was doing my best to tend to him and to be a good mother. He was getting sweeter by the day. While breastfeeding, as I held him, I would caress his soft skin, thinking about our future. I would not leave him behind.

Bijan moved out of the bedroom, claiming the baby made it hard to sleep, the lack of which might affect his looks. Waking groggy and working tired might age his "moneymaker"...his handsome face. He needed his beauty sleep.

This arrangement suited me fine, odd as it was. I no longer bothered to understand Bijan. He had been willing to go to the moon and back to become a father but was behaving like a sperm donor. Busy with his career, he'd never changed one diaper or fed the baby late at night.

The more time I spent with the little one, the more dedicated I became. I had never imagined motherhood could be this fulfilling. My purpose was to love, support, and take care of my child. My entire focus was on him. James became my refuge, my reason to live and grow stronger through the bitter days of life with Bijan.

I often thanked God for the gift of my son. It was almost as if I needed him more than he needed me. Just like my mother, I would give my child love and security. What about Bijan? I was still waiting for him to be a good husband. How likely was it he would take his responsibilities as a father seriously?

I was spending most of my time at home or visiting my parents. Dad adored my son, at times, it seemed, more than he adored me. It didn't matter. To share James with my family was a blessing that nearly didn't happen.

When our son reached six months, Bijan planned a European vacation with his married friends, Shain, an Iranian singer, and his wife. I had reservations about spending a month traveling with Shain's wife as we had little in common. I would have to make the best of it and expect to be surprised.

I was hesitant to leave my child, but Mom insisted, saying, "You look tired and thin, a vacation will be good for you." Little did she know the baby had nothing to do with my rundown appearance. My mother was the only person I let care for James.

The vacation started with ten days in Rome. I fell in love with Italy, the people, the food, the beauty of the country itself. Who wouldn't fall in love with this gorgeous country? Our itinerary was hectic, so we hired a local English-speaking guide. We asked to see out-of-the-way, non-tourist spots. We visited Naples, Capri, Sorrento and other incredible towns.

At our 200-year-old hotel, marble statues and a beautiful garden patio surrounded us. The smell of flowers could feed your soul. Guests were seated in antique chairs with tables covered in linens so delicate and beautiful one would be hesitant to touch them, never mind use them for a meal.

The beauty of Rome was surpassed only by the deliciousness of its food, which was as if Gods had prepared it. Within a week, I had gained three kilos but was not surprised. I ate without end.

We visited Vatican City - Citta Del Vaticano - where the Pope, leader of all Catholics, lived. The Vatican is said to be built over the tomb of Saint Peter.

Beneath the church was a dimly lit mausoleum with narrow and cold walkways where the mummified bodies of previous popes lay, each with its glory and history. As I wondered about their lives and the eras in which they lived, I felt disquieted to be among the dead.

As irresistible as eating is in Italy, shopping was a close second. The Italian talent for fashion had me feeling like a child with a blank check on her birthday. Designer Emilio Pucci was my favorite. At his boutique, I indulged in gorgeous dresses and accessories.

While strolling the Via Veneto, I chose shoes and handbags. I could spend weeks shopping. I reflected on a rare sense of real happiness afterward, relaxing outside a coffee shop with a perfect cappuccino and delicious Dolce pastry.

Unfortunately, it came time to leave Italy for Paris, where our hotel was within walking distance of the main center.

As soon as we freshened up, it was time for a walk on Champs Elise, Paris' most famous street. Me, on the Rue de Champs Elise, imagine that.

Everything seemed like a dream and even more like the movies, where so often I had seen little cafes and bistros crowded with tourists and locals. The smell of French coffee permeated the air.

The next day, it was off to the Du Louvre Musee. Every piece of art was phenomena, including Venus, the Mona Lisa, Napoleon's dining room. A tour of French history would require more than a day. I hungered to see every detail, and endless questions went unsatisfied, especially with the language barrier.

One of our more adventurous outings took us to Pigalle, the city's "red milieu" district. The blatant sexuality, from hookers in sexy lingerie to sex shops selling all sorts of weird gadgets and penises in all shapes and colors, was a first for me. Iran had nothing even close.

Seeing leather outfits with long boots, whips, handcuffs and other extreme toys, made my jaw drop. We took advantage of the novelty and inserted coins into machines that ran short clips of porn movies.

All the excitement made us hungry. One little bistro still had its lights on, but the chef made it clear that it was after business hours. Realizing he was dealing with a few hungry tourists, he put together a large tray, proudly placed it and a bottle of red wine on the table with a "Voila, Bon appetite!" and walked away.

I could not believe my eyes. French bread and cheeses, lettuce, olives, shrimp, and tomato with fresh basil, all of which I craved, filled the tray.

However, arranged artistically in the center were long fried sausages. All I saw were the fake penises. It was impossible to eat. My husband and our friends had a good laugh, but I ate bread, cheese, and a plate of salad. I won't soon forget that night or the bistro in Pigalle, Paris.

The following morning, we set off to stroll in Saint Jermaine Rue, a plaza where, on any corner, you could find young, poor artists, mostly students, with big dreams.

Later, seeing the La Ture Eifel, I could not help but marvel at its wonder of cold metal, reaching to the sky. To think many Parisians despised it at first.

The guide told us the tower was cordoned off beyond a certain height to prevent suicides. But the view from the height we were allowed to climb was still worth the effort. The panorama gave me a glimpse of the ultimate freedom for which I longed.

We enjoyed dinner and a show at Le Lido de Paris, but there was much more to see than we had time for. I was thankful to have gotten to see Notre Dame Cathedral, one of the most beautiful in all of Europe, with its dramatic towers, spire, stained glass and statuary with breathtaking, precious pieces of art.

Our two weeks was soon over. We would next arrive in Spain, then on to England, and finally, home to Tehran.

Twenty

Bijan received a telegram when we were just leaving Paris. He would have to be in Turkey to begin shooting much sooner than planned. Our friends suggested that I continue the trip with them, but Bijan did not agree.

"Quelle surprise," I thought. His excuse was that this trip was our honeymoon, and he wanted me to accompany him to Turkey.

In private, I told him: "I don't want to go to Turkey, to walk the streets wondering if passersby were among those who massacred my ancestors.

"Have you forgotten the Armenian Genocide at the hands of the Turks? It would be like taking a Jewish person to Auschwitz for vacation. I won't go. If I can't continue with our friends to Spain and England, then I'd rather go back to Tehran."

Bijan looked at me with amazement. "It has been almost sixty years, when will you forget it?"

I snapped, "Never! As long as blood runs through my veins, I will carry the memory with me, and I won't let my children forget it either, or their children. The Turks need to admit to the barbaric act they committed against my people."

Bijan could not understand why suddenly I became so anti-Turk. I tried to explain, "I never expected to go to Turkey. I wasn't supposed to go with you. It was not part of our vacation.

You usually don't take me with you when you work. Why this time?"

I paused for a moment and then continued, "You don't want me to go with them because you won't be there to know every detail of where I go or what I do every moment. After marrying you, then bearing your child, I had hoped this possessiveness would heal.

"I would love to see Spain, experience its delicious cuisine, bodegas, red wine, and Flamenco dancers, oh and the sound of Spanish guitars played by masters.

"I want to walk by Number Ten Downing Street in London, see Hyde Park and spend the day at Madame Trousseau's Wax Museum. I want to shop at Harrods and see the countryside. That was our itinerary. Please tell me why I can't go with them."

He replied, "Regardless of your nationalistic speech, you are going with me." Pausing, he asked, "Being so patriotic, why did you marry a Muslim?" His words hurt more than bullets could have.

In my defense, I wish I would have said, "Because I was afraid of Muslims, just like my ancestors were."

He said I had no option but to go with him. Moreover, he had the passports and the tickets. In a few days, we would say goodbye to our friends and leave Paris for Istanbul, Turkey.

಄ৡৣ಄

Sitting on the tarmac, I began to think about my heritage. In 1965, as a Girl Scout, we commemorated the 50th anniversary of genocide with a candle vigil followed by a ceremony for the souls of those who died from 1913-15 as well as survivors of rape, plunder, and torture during the massive genocide.

Areas of present-day Turkey had belonged to Armenia. It would not be an easy country to visit.

Emotions continued to overwhelm me after landing and checking in at the hotel. I started to cry. A few hours before, I was having lunch in Paris. Now I had to have dinner in Istanbul. The cultural, historical, and emotional shock was like a knife in my heart.

During the days that followed, I accompanied Bijan to the movie's production studios, filming locations, and meeting sites. One night, an Iranian actress, Parvin, invited us to dinner at a seaside restaurant. I had heard she was dating the Turkish co-star of the movie. Bijan wasn't eager to go. He asked me to call and excuse us, saying I had a sudden headache.

It angered me that he was not man enough to pick up the phone and tell her the truth.

When I called her, the hotel receptionist said she had already left. Happy inside, but keeping cool, I told Bijan that it was too late to cancel. A trace of disappointment crossed his face, and he seemed agitated. But why? A simple dinner with colleagues shouldn't be this unpleasant.

I knew Bijan had dated Parvin years before. Was he jealous of seeing her with another? No, that couldn't be it. Each had dated many others since the breakup.

Was he worried that another man might be at our table? Bijan was a complicated character, never predictable.

I was looking forward to a fun night out, rather than spending it in the hotel watching TV, without understanding a word.

Conscious of Bijan's attitude - and for my sake, I dressed casually in a pair of dark blue jeans I'd bought in Paris, with soft and fluffy white top. My hair was loose around my shoulders, and I wore light makeup. I still felt gorgeous and was sure Bijan was eating his heart out.

Arriving at the restaurant, a happy Parvin greeted us and stood to hug and kiss us before introducing the handsome man beside her as Samir, one of the top ten Turkish movie stars.

He was a Turk. Maybe his grandfather was the one who killed my grandfather. Should I hold him responsible? I asked myself how I would have felt if he were to hate me for what my grandfather did?

To my surprise, there was a translator at our table so our Farsi and Turkish languages could be understood. Apparently, no one spoke English. Amused, I realized that our communication was going to be quite funny.

Dinner was delicious. Any seafood you can imagine was on the table, as well as several local side dishes, called mazzah, including salads made of lettuce, cucumber, and very juicy tomatoes, fresh herbs and pilaf with saffron. There was also Turkish vodka, which when mixed with water would turn the color of milk. It tasted horrible.

In a corner, a band played Turkish music, and a belly dancer was moving like a snake as if her body had no bones. She slithered from table to table, dancing mostly for the men. We were all having fun, laughing, eating, and dancing and Bijan, surprisingly, seemed to be enjoying it too.

Samir made a comment, to which the translator turned to my husband and said, "Samir wants to congratulate you for having such a drop-dead beautiful wife."

Oh, no. This could not be good, judging from Bijan's history of anger when men complimented me. I quickly prayed that the night would continue peacefully. To my disbelief, Bijan stayed calm and thanked Samir.

After the dinner, Samir stood to accompany me to the restroom, like a proper host. With eyes opened wide, Bijan watched us walk away. Samir waited and accompanied me back to the table. I considered it a courtesy, but doubt Bijan looked at it that way. He was likely sure this man was trying to charm me and make a pass.

On the way to our table, a photographer took our photo while we walked next to each other. I worried that Bijan would take this wrong. The picture was developed and brought to our table.

The Turkish actor asked to keep it, but Bijan requested he write a few words on the back and give it to us as a memento. It seemed a calculated move on Bijan's part to keep even my picture out of another man's possession.

The night went peacefully. At about two in the morning, we thanked our hosts for the lovely evening and headed toward our hotel. Later, in bed, I told Bijan I wanted to return home.

I missed James, and even though he was safe in my parents' kind hands, I couldn't bear to be away from him. It had been more than a month since I had seen my child. Bijan immediately agreed, as if I had read his mind.

Two days later, I flew back to Tehran. Amir, my brother-in-law, greeted me at the Mehrabad airport. From there, it was on to my parents' house. From the moment I entered the house, I was at ease and completely relaxed. My whole family was there, except Edwin, who was living in England. Home is certainly a unique place in the world.

A month had passed, and there was my son in my mother's arms. I stepped toward him excitedly, with open arms, eager to hold him, smell him, and squeeze him tight.

He turned away, gripping my mother with both hands. He had forgotten me and was afraid. My heart broke. I tried sharing toys I had bought on the trip. After a few minutes of play, he sought my mother's arms again.

The next day, I took him home. At almost seven months, James was the cutest and sweetest baby in the world to me, and I intended to restore his attachment to his mother, once more.

Twenty-One

On January 22, 1977, we celebrated James' first birthday. Our only guests were my in-laws. My parents never socialized with my in-laws. In fact, my father never stepped foot in my house.

My mother-in-law gave a colorful wooden riding horse to her first male grandchild. James was so happy moving back and forth on it; he refused to dismount. I was very proud of him. At only one year, he was bilingual in Armenian and Farsi and able to distinguish between both languages.

Life continued, and the distance between my husband and I grew larger by the day. Bijan surprised me with a beautiful set of diamond earrings, "A small token of my appreciation for you giving me a son," he said.

I could decorate my body with expensive gifts, but my heart remained cold and empty. Only one special jewel could fill the emptiness at my core.

We were two strangers living under the same roof, occasionally having sex; we had nothing in common. What angered me most was the realization of the truth about his character. He had no respect for women; they were mere sex objects. I wondered if he understood that a woman had given him the gift of life.

Aside from our son, there was no reason for me to stay and share my life with Bijan. I did not love him, and such self-betrayal is hard. I desperately needed to leave. I was miserable, yearning for a divorce, but I knew there would be a war over James.

Bijan was using our son like a gun. Whenever I asked for a divorce, he pointed the gun at my temple, threatening that I would never get my son.

My options were limited. I did not want to return to my parents' home to live there after all I had done. Acting was my only income option, which I loved to do. Indeed, I missed it very much. I knew very well that Bijan would do anything to stop me, anything!

One evening after dinner, although I knew Bijan would try to sabotage my movie career, I decided to open my heart without fear of being hurt again.

After putting James to bed, I returned to the dining room table, lit a cigarette, then asked Bijan to pay attention and listen to me because I wanted to discuss something important. Looking startled and puzzled, "What is it this time?" he asked.

I started, "We've been married a few years, but each passing month of our life together brings more proof that it was wrong for us to marry. You and I are very different. I cannot make you happy. Although you often say I am the wife you always wished for, your actions prove the opposite. It's obvious you can't make me happy either.

"So, why are we torturing each other? Why do we live together? You might find a woman who would make you happy, and I might find the right man. Please, I beg you to agree to a divorce. For heaven's sake, why can't you see we aren't made for each other?

"Everything with you is by force. To marry by force, to have a child by force, to live with you by force, how long do you think you can force me to stay with you?"

After listening, Bijan replied calmly and coldly, "I told you before; I didn't marry you to divorce you. Thus, I will never let you go and take my son with you."

I knew he would use anything and everything against me as soon as he felt he was losing his power and control. I preferred not to continue talking. I did not want him to get angry, which usually ended with him hurting me.

We never had a logical, quiet discussion. I dreaded that my child might witness our fights and his mother's pain. My husband's hands were his tongue for any conversation, especially when it didn't go his way.

I had to be patient and wait for the right time, not knowing when it would come. Freedom would be the day I could take my son and leave Bijan, forever.

Maybe one day I would meet my soul mate, be complete and be able to put Bijan and tormenting memories of him behind me. I wondered what Bernard was doing. However, I had to concentrate on my son and myself.

Days went by as my miserable life continued. My husband continued to act in movies and tighten his grip on me. Despite my hopes, I knew he would never change.

My brother had left Iran in 1975 for England. That gave me the hope that I could take James and run away to England without ever letting my husband know our whereabouts.

Unfortunately, the country's regulations meant I needed my husband's official written permission to travel abroad. Women were treated as children, incapable of making sound decisions for own lives. Asking him to sign the papers was out of the question.

Circumstances were against me and my plan. I was desperately trying to break free of the cage Bijan had me living in and fly away in the hope of finding my lost happy life.

Meanwhile, rumors about Iran's instability were growing. One could sense the push into an unknown future. Something was wrong, but exactly what that was couldn't be pinpointed. Above all, we frequently heard Khomeini's name.

I wished I had paid more attention to national politics. Who was this Khomeini? Making inquiries, I learned he was a Muslim cleric, exiled by the Shah for anti-regime activities almost fifteen years prior. He avoided a death sentence because of his position. Instead, the court exiled him to Iraq.

I recall President Jimmy Carter and his wife, Rosalyn, were in Iran on New Year's Eve of 1978. During a speech at the Iranian Royal Palace, President Carter said, "Iran is the most stable country in the Middle East."

Those words remain unforgettable to this day. That same month, demonstrations against the Shah, which had started in October of 1977, intensified until they paralyzed the country from August through December.

By mid-January of 1979, the Shah would be exiled as the last Persian monarch, leaving his supporters to fend for themselves. The decades since have revealed that Carter may have known more than he let on.

In that same month, an article disparaging Khomeini's character and morals caused an immense uproar amongst radical Muslims, who called the writing an insult to Khomeini and Islam. It began in the city of Qom, south of Tehran, home to Iran's second most significant shrine, Mashhad - the burial place of the eighth Shiite Imam Reza.

The city had many Islamic schools and streets filled with Talabe, the Farsi name for students studying to become

Mullahs. On the few occasions that we had to stop in Qom on our way to other cities, I never felt comfortable among the sea of women hidden under Islamic mandated chadors.

Covered head-to-toe in black, with even their faces masked, they appeared as flocks of crows. Covering the body was one thing, but my question was, "How can they cover their mind, brain, thought processes, free will, and human rights?"

The unrest in Qom had resulted in several deaths and the closure of its bazaars, set in to motion a cycle of demonstrations, with crowds shouting Khomeini's name, a name that was an ever-increasing rallying cry. Many Iranians, including me, wondered what he wanted. What could he possibly do for our country?

In August 1978, we decided to spend a few weeks at the Caspian Sea with a group of friends. I had always loved it there, where I could walk barefoot along the shore, dig my feet into the sand and listen to the waves as they soothed my tormented soul.

We stayed at a villa that had a fantastic view of the sea. We spent our days swimming, sunbathing, waterskiing, eating the freshest seafood, and enjoying restaurants and nightclubs, until the 19th, when we finally packed to head back to Tehran.

Fidgeting with the car's radio knob on the drive, I realized programming on every station was suddenly interrupted by horrifying breaking news. The announcer reported Cinema Rex in Abadan had been set on fire, resulting in a hellish inferno, where an estimated 300 to 400 people had been locked inside, burned alive.

Bijan, hands shaking and unable to control the car, pulled over in shock. Neither could I believe what I had just heard. I changed stations, only to confirm that all were reporting on the fire. After our return, rumors blaming the government began to spread. This mass murder pushed the people to total madness.

Personally, I saw no evidence or possible motivation for the current government to do such a thing and could not agree with those who believed this idea. A strange wave was spreading silently throughout the country, as if a giant snake, moving underground, had reached its prey without attracting attention. That snake was Khomeini.

Fifteen years prior, he had brought the country to the verge of anarchy but had failed. This time, wounded but much more dangerous and bloodthirsty, he was gaining ground. Why had the Shah forgiven this Satan? If only he had taken this threat more seriously.

To my surprise, Britain's BBC radio seemed to generously and continually broadcast Khomeini's provocative messages, reaching Iranian Muslims with warnings of the Shah's threat to Islam and their duty to stand up and fight against him and his followers. It seemed the radio network had become an Islamic loudspeaker, which one might find atop every mosque.

Why was the BBC broadcasting in Farsi in support of Khomeini and against Iran's government, in particular, the Shah and the many Iranians who were against this insane movement? Did the outsiders have an agenda?

I'd studied Iranian history at school and knew Britain already had taken more than enough from us. How much more did they want, a new oil contract or some other exploitation of our resources?

From my view, it was another immoral and shameless interference from a foreign government. If someone could have opened the curtain, for sure we could have seen other players behind the anarchy in my country, Britain was not the only one.

The nightmare we were witnessing continued beyond control with massive strikes, those by students closing universities and those by workers hurting an already ailing economy. Finally, the government stepped in, positioning army tanks on the streets to secure and maintain the peace. The Iranian Oil Company's workers strike was hindering the country's most important and valuable source of income: oil.

The Shah appeared on television to promise he would do his best to satisfy the majority. He was asking for time and warning of anarchy and losing the county's unity and independence. I remember him saying, "We can't let Iran be divided into several self-ruled states. The unity of the country as a whole will be in danger."

I thought this strategy was wrong; the Shah shouldn't have given in. What was to come next would prove me right. The speech backfired, giving more power and ammunition to the opposition. They sensed weakness and started to exert even more pressure, mainly using religion against the Shah, his government, and members of the Royal family.

Unfortunately, the mass of Iranians, as in most countries, are lacking basic knowledge and a common understanding of how the world functions or the political aspects of ruling a country. This lack of awareness gave more power to instigators to control the people.

When dealing with an uneducated person, one thinks, "Well, this person doesn't know better." But when an educated person has fallen for propaganda against his country, you have to wonder what happened. Why, suddenly, was everyone against the regime and the Shah? From where had so many opposition groups come?

At times, while driving in the streets of Tehran, we would be stuck between different demonstrations, posters bearing

Khomeini's name and image in almost every pair of hands. On the big placards one could read, "The Shah must go!" or "Down with the Shah and the Pahlavi Dynasty!"

Watching the wild crowds from the car, angry, aggressive, and behaving like wounded animals, I saw old people and children marching, shouting, and tearing their clothes. It was depressing to see their faces, with unfamiliar features, seemingly foreign.

Who were they and from where had they come? Did they realize what they were doing, or that they were following a dangerous "leader" like marionettes being controlled by their strings?

The day Tehran was ruined is branded into my memory. Driving the morning streets was like an episode of *The Twilight Zone.*

My beautiful city had been destroyed. Metal doors of banks were torn off, shops, liquor stores, and boutiques were burned down, cars, still in lanes, were ablaze; movie theaters, cabarets, and nightclubs were demolished as if a bomb had exploded and burned everything to ashes.

The city was unrecognizable. Through it all, those unfamiliar faces were in the streets. From where had they come?

Twenty-Two

James was almost two and half years old when I got pregnant again. Under different circumstances, it would have been a joyous occasion, but to have another child with Bijan would be like swallowing poison.

Honestly, I'd rather drink the poison. I convinced Bijan that we had to leave the country, the situation was getting dangerous, and I didn't want to be carrying a child in a foreign country with an unknown future.

He agreed to the abortion and maybe leaving Iran. The abortion was a lesser sin than bringing a child into this hell, something I would expect more unforgivable by God than the abortion itself.

The situation worsened, so I started to pressure my husband to leave the country. The movie industry – now considered satanic and against Islam - had collapsed, which meant there was no work for Bijan. Members of the industry were looked upon as servants of the Shah, to be destroyed.

To my surprise, Bijan agreed to contact my brother in England to arrange for us to go there. Meanwhile, on Guadalupe Island, leaders of world oil's fabled Seven Sisters - Exxon, Shell, Mobil, Texaco, British Petroleum, Standard Oil of California and Gulf, gathered to decide the fate of Iran. Their resolution was to support Khomeini and destroy the Pahlavi Monarchy, the Shah, and, in a word, Iran.

On a cold and rainy day in autumn of 1978, we left for England. Leaving my family was one of the most painful goodbyes ever. I constantly wondered, "Will I be able to see them again?" It was heartbreaking to see my son start to cry along with the family, without him even understanding why.

Dad took his grandson into his arms and held him tight for quite a while. Putting him down, Dad left the room and could be heard sobbing from behind the door. I asked my family not to come to the airport, to save us further sadness of our bitter farewell. I prayed God would keep them safe until the day we could reunite.

We landed at London Heathrow, claimed our luggage, and then we approached the immigration checkpoint. The anxious faces of Iranian passengers, who like me, had run away from Iran in the hope they might one day return, crowded the lines. The faces of immigration officers, by contrast, were cold and stern, with little compassion in their glassy eyes.

I overheard the conversation of a woman in front of me in line. The agent was questioning her about her reasons for coming to London and how long she planned to stay. She replied that she had planned to stay with her two sons, who were University of London students.

The official ignored her long-term visa validation and stamped her passport for only a month. In tears, her imploring failed to change the officer's mind.

Witnessing what just happened, I feared this man could return us to Tehran, immediately. He motioned me to approach. Bijan couldn't speak English. Handing over our passports, I awaited his questions. They were the same: "Why did you come to London?" and "How long are you planning to stay?"

For a moment, a brutally honest answer came to mind. "I am here because of your country and others' interference and propaganda are destroying my country."

I thought better of it, knowing it would likely land me back in Tehran. I replied, "To be with my brother, spend some time with him, and travel throughout England."

He checked our tickets, asking, "If this is the case, why do you have a one-way ticket?"

A quick answer came to mind. "Because from England, we plan to visit other European countries."

He finally stamped our passports, allowing a six-month stay. What he was thinking, I will never know. But I had succeeded. Bijan, of course, was relieved and thrilled. I reflected on my independent nature. If I had relied on Bijan, we would likely be on a plane back to Iran.

From London, we taxied seventy-seven miles to Ramsgate, in Kent, where my brother, Edwin lived. The driver probably thought we were crazy taking such a long and expensive cab ride, but we needed the convenience. We were tired, physically and mentally drained.

We were not on vacation; we were on a life altering path, not knowing how it would end. In the following days and weeks, we kept busy looking for a place to live, enrolling in school, finding James a nearby kindergarten while following the news on Iran over radio and TV. It was never positive. Frequent calls home revealed the situation had worsened.

On January 16, 1979, while watching the news in shock and disbelief, we saw the Shah was leaving the country. No, no, I thought to myself, you shouldn't leave, if you go it will be over, for you, for us, for millions of Iranians. You have to stay, you are the captain of the ship, and you should be the last to abandon.

I had never before seen the Shah in tears, but I did on that day. Every man breaks at some point. His generals and soldiers surrounded him, kissing his hand. One soldier, while crying, said, "I wish I were blind, so as not to see this day."

Iranians safe in England were crying with them as I am sure, were many across Iran. What would happen now? Was his health issue that serious or was he abandoning his people and country? What might he know that we did not?

By February 1979, Khomeini headed to Iran on Air France. The French government seemed to be extending hospitality equal to the BBC's. I just could not understand. What was wrong with these countries? I watched in horror his interview en route.

A reporter had asked him "What sort of feelings do you have upon returning to your country after almost fifteen years?" His response was a shrug of his shoulders and the word "Nothing."

Did I see and hear that right? "Nothing?" If he felt nothing for the country, why he was returning? I think his reason was for his political interests and possibly a religious assignment to destroy the entire country and the people who had built it during the previous decades.

In October 1979, we heard the news of the Shah traveling to the United States for medical treatment for cancer. One cancer called Khomeini was not enough; now this one was going to finish him.

Months of traveling back and forth were extremely difficult for the King whose days were numbered. The travel would have been taxing for a healthy person and now our beloved king, living in the royal palace in a country with three thousand years of history and culture had become a rolling stone, a very lonely king.

Not long after, we watched in disbelief as the U.S. Embassy in Tehran was attacked. People were climbing walls and gates and jumping into what they thought would be safety within the embassy. Guards withdrew into the compound as well, locking the entrances behind them. Such efforts were in vain. Soon embassy employees were arrested and transferred to another location.

You could see the fear on their faces, surrounded by an angry crowd, yelling "Dirty spies!" The attackers humiliated and cursed them, holding them hostage in hopes of exchanging them for the Shah.

If I were the Shah, I would never return to Iran. Who could condemn his departure? He had done so much for Iran, bringing it out of the relative Stone Age to become one of the most powerful and advanced countries in the region.

Perhaps if Iran were not Islamic, money and power hungry foreign leaders wouldn't have been able to cause harm. And if Iran didn't have oil, maybe they would have left us alone. But as it was, they seemed to want our oil and our blood.

ॐ ❀ ॐ

My life in England started early each morning. First, I had to take James, who was almost three years old, to early kindergarten. Then I would rush to my school through the afternoon, pick up my child, then grocery shop on the way home.

At home, after spending time with James, I prepared dinner. Finally, after Bijan and my son went to bed, I would study. This was my routine.

My marital problems continued. Life in England was like exile to Bijan, and his disposition worsened. He was becoming angrier and was repeatedly beating me. If not for James, I would have left Bijan in a heartbeat.

As it was, I would spend my life wondering where my child was, what was he doing, asking myself if he was okay, or if he was happy and thousands of other questions.

I knew I would never be happy without my child. I was dreaming of the day we could both escape and live happily and free from under Bijan's potentially deadly shadow.

My life and my country were upside down. Since Khomeini's return, anarchy ruled. The number of executions, kidnappings and terror campaigns became too numerous to count. There was not a single day that passed without executions, imprisonment or inhumane torture. Iranian blood flowed.

In late Spring of '79, my husband decided to return to Iran. When confronted about our son's future, he answered: "My son's blood is not brighter than all those kids living in Iran."

Out of anger and frustration, I asked, "You, too, want to go kiss Khomeini's ass? I am not going back. I will stay here in England." As usual, the anger and beating started, leaving me bruised, physically and mentally.

Still, I tried to convince him that it was a big mistake to return. The more I implored, the more he rushed toward Tehran, threatening to take my son and go.

In a call to my mother, I told her of Bijan's decision to return to Iran. She went ballistic, "Have you lost your minds?" She explained that my husband being a movie actor, married to a Christian woman, also an actor, would make us an obvious target of the Islamic government.

She said Bijan's decision would put our lives in danger and warned of likely immediate arrest at the airport. She said if we weren't thinking of ourselves, we should consider our son. She ended the call by saying I was crazy to come back. I had proof enough of my craziness in having married Bijan.

By summer we were packed to leave the U.K. My brother was also leaving, heading to Switzerland. At Heathrow, I bought a few small bottles of liquor, unbeknownst to my husband. He would not have dared to carry alcohol to Tehran under the new Islamic regulations.

Despite my mother's warning, I didn't care, thinking if agents found it, they would just confiscate it. As a social drinker only, I wondered why I would buy alcohol to take to Tehran, knowing the danger? Was I rebelling and looking for trouble? Possibly, still, the contraband went into the oversized shoulder bag filled with my son's necessities for the trip.

I took a window seat. Bijan sat next to me, while James slept in my arms. As the plane ascended higher and higher, my hopes of freedom descended ever lower.

Twenty-Three

We landed at the Mehrabad Airport in Tehran. Walking towards pass control, I was already sorry. I wanted to grab my son, run back to the plane, and go back to England. Another impossible dream.

The airport was not the same as it had been when we left for England just six months before. Khomeini posters - and ones with other faces unknown to me as yet - covered the walls. Chadors hid women from head to toe. Khomeini's "elite" army stood guard, monitoring everyone and everything.

We handed over our passports. I noticed the controller called another person over and showed him our passports, mumbling something into his ear. Without a word to us he took our passports and disappeared into a nearby room. Half an hour later, two guards with guns appeared and ordered us to follow them.

I looked at Bijan. He was pale. Without pity, I mumbled, "Don't forget, your son's blood is not brighter than all other kids here." He did not reply.

They took us to a small room at the back of the airport, where a mullah and a few other people sat behind a desk. All along, I was carrying bottles of scotch and cognac. From a huge poster on the wall behind them, was Khomeini's face staring down with fury.

For two hours in that room, they questioned and insulted us. James was half-asleep in my arms and didn't know what was going on. It seemed as if they would never let us out or would send us to jail, immediately. I couldn't resist an honest answer when one of the inspectors asked why we returned: "Because of the stupidity of my husband. I didn't want to come back at all."

Bijan was clearly frightened. Despite the fear in his eyes, I thought he deserved it. He was the one who insisted on coming back to this Islamic hell. Perhaps they appreciated that he wanted to return. The inspector asked him, "You are a real Muslim?"

After hours of interrogation, they asked for our address and allowed us to leave. They had thoroughly searched our luggage, but for some reason, did not check the large handbag in which I had placed the mini liquor bottles. Bijan would have fainted had he known.

On the concourse, crowded with people waiting to greet passengers, we spotted Bijan's brothers. We drove out of the airport immediately, fearing they may change their minds and arrest us.

Finally, within the safety of my in-laws' home, I called my family to let them know we had arrived and that I missed them, promising to visit the next day.

Later that night, while discussing the current climate with Bijan's parents, he suddenly said, "I wish I had shot of scotch. After everything, we went through today; only a drink will soothe me."

Without a word, I took the bottles out of the travel bag for him to see, asking, "Which kind would you prefer?" A range of expressions crossed his face, from excitement, fright, curiosity, disbelief, even a hint of anger. Ultimately, he was relieved to have a drink and did not challenge me.

We stayed at my in-laws while looking for a place of our own. Within a few months, we moved into a new home. However, given the conditions of life in Tehran, it was not a happy occasion; gone was our former way of life.

Iran seemed dead. It was impossible for people like us, who had nothing to do with this madness, to remain sane and live as if nothing had happened.

Meanwhile, Bijan sought work. Acting was out of the question. The movie industry had been declared anti-Islam. Every single art and cultural activity had been banned and shut down. It was as if life itself closed down with a big lock hanging from its gate with the keys in Khomeini's hand.

We had lost a domestic war and now lived as prisoners of this demon, Khomeini. Only in the safety of our homes could we share information or discuss political affairs.

There was no middle ground; people were either totally for or totally against the new regime. Every friend of ours was trying to leave the country. There was a huge exodus of high-ranking army members, movie industry professionals, singers, writers, doctors, lawyers and religious minorities.

Meanwhile, chaos reigned. There was no organized law, rules or regulations. Society was a symphony of individuals playing their music, where there should have been a conductor, were Islamic guards pointing guns.

As for me, it was déjà-vu. I had been through a similar overthrow when I had gotten married, which resulted in the loss of most of my rights and my freedom as a woman. Now another revolution had taken over the rest of my world.

Meanwhile, to everyone's surprise, a small downtown theater started daily performances. The troupe was thrilled when my husband signed a contract to join them. In better days, he would have been insulted had anyone asked him to perform there. As it was, he started appearing twice a day, and within a month, three times a day.

Audiences packed the theater, enjoying their screen heroes who were within their reach, touchable and real, not to mention their last source of art and entertainment.

The excellent income was a relief. I could breathe and just be with my son without being in constant fear of Bijan's mood swings and violent outbursts. But my husband's success was another wedge between us. Most of the time, he was at the theater, performing or rehearsing.

Knowing the regime could not be trusted, we stopped saving money at the bank; instead, we stowed it throughout the house. We hid cash in the washing machine, the dryer, the dishwasher, freezer, and even the oven. The fear of thieves was nothing compared to our fear of the regime confiscating his earnings.

Through it all, we got together about twice a month with those friends who had not fled. Usually, we gathered for a dinner party, where everyone would exchange the latest news, now solely related to politics.

Everyone had become a pundit. At times, conversations would become heated about Khomeini, the mullahs, the Mujahedin Khalgh, the communists, Islam, the Shah, the army, the lefties, the Cherikhaye Fadaei or whatever issue arose.

I found the men's conversation more fascinating than the topics the women discussed. I couldn't resist joining them and sharing my point of view. Bijan disapproved, of course, preferring I stay within the group of women. When I would try to discuss my motivation, something you would think a husband would understand by now, it ended in the usual unresolved argument.

ಐ෨<ಐ

By summer of 1980, my still-miserable life was getting nowhere. Bijan was mostly absent, spending his time God-knows-where. Meanwhile, the Islamic regime continued spreading its web throughout the country. I was alone against both. One would beat me if I disobeyed, the other would lock me up saying it was Allah's will.

Growing despair had me thinking about approaching my father with the truth. I fantasized about describing my living hell, revealing Bijan's beatings and verbal abuse and my feeling as if I was slowly dying. If only I could let Dad know that I wanted a divorce and to escape with my son.

But I could never bring myself to do it. Somehow, I knew I had to carry the pain alone, having created this mess on my own. I would find a way out, however impossible it seemed.

To my surprise, the manager of the theater where Bijan performed asked if I would like to join the group. Thrilled, of course, I said yes. But then he approached Bijan, who completely lost it. There would be no way I could act again.

Twenty-Four

As days passed, people continued to lose hope, and many lost their lives. Khomeini strengthened, continuing the bloodshed that seemed to fuel his existence.

On a summer afternoon in late July, Bijan had a rare day off. I told him I wanted to take James to visit my brother in Switzerland for a month. He agreed. Yes, he agreed!

I wondered what motive he had for letting me leave. He had to have a motive. Otherwise, he would have forbidden it. Whatever it was, I didn't care. I was thrilled to escape, even for a short while, from my sworn enemies, him and the regime.

Two weeks later, our plane landed in Zurich where my brother and his girlfriend, Manuela, were waiting. The difference between two cultures just a few-hour-flight apart was stark. It was almost as if I had returned to the freedom of pre-revolution Iran.

I felt this experience was necessary for James as well. Though just a little more than four years old, he had witnessed the torment of his parents' relationship.

The trip was much-needed therapy for me. Perhaps my son needed it even more, despite missing his father. He would run and play in the park in front of my brother's apartment as I listened to his laughter from a nearby bench. He seemed genuinely happy.

Edwin and Manuela took us to various cities in Switzerland. Geneva was my favorite. Besides its architectural beauty, it was home to many diplomats and those who worked for international organizations.

At Lake Geneva, I saw the magnificent Jet d'Eau, a large fountain lit at night, pumping its water 140 meters into the air.

The language was a barrier for me at restaurants, parks, and the theater. The locals called their language "Schweitzer Deutch," Swiss German. The younger generation had a better understanding of English.

One day while strolling and shopping with my brother and Manuela, I pulled my shirt up a bit above my jeans to scratch my waist. Suddenly, James rushed towards me, pulled down my shirt and remarked, "Don't you know people can see your waist. Dad said when he is not around I have to be the man and take care of you." I was speechless.

Manuela could not understand Armenian, but still, her face showed surprise. Edwin didn't comment, but I could see he was thinking, "Like father, like son."

I wasn't pleased. It hurt to see my son acting like his father, the last thing I wanted. He was only four, yet his reaction to me showing one inch of my waist was extreme. It seemed as if I was raising another Bijan. Nevertheless, the incident opened my eyes. I refused to let him turn into a monster. Dealing with one was enough.

I would hate to witness the day James followed in his father's footsteps. He may become a creature with no respect for women, who would dominate, control, torture and brutally abuse them.

He wouldn't know anything about loving and cherishing a woman. He would think they weren't good for anything except for sex and being the ones to cook, clean, and deliver babies.

James was too precious to me to ignore what had just happened. It was a wake-up call. From then on, I had another cause for which to fight, besides my freedom. I would never let my son become like his father.

About a week before our departure, I had settled into a routine of daily shopping, an incurable habit, then and now. After one such day, I was in the kitchen, preparing Iranian food for my brother, when he came running in a panic. Taking my hand, he nearly dragged me to the living room and turned on the TV.

I couldn't understand his sudden strange behavior, besides he knew I didn't know German. Before my questions came, I saw the news was on, then suddenly realized the places and language were familiar. I just sat down, trying to understand why Iran was in the news again.

At first, I thought perhaps the Islamic regime was doomed, and there had been a coup in Iran, kicking the Ayatollah Khomeini and his guards out of the country.

How wrong I was. I saw army troops, tanks, machine guns, grenades, and missiles in what was southern Iran. Several times, travel had taken me to cities in the region. I recognized the oil refineries.

My brother turned to me and spoke in English instead of Armenian so that James, who was in the room playing with his new toys would not be able to understand what he was about to say. In tears, his voice breaking, Edwin said, "Linda, Iraq has declared war against Iran. Their troops have entered the country, and there have been casualties."

It didn't make any sense. How was it possible? Saddam Hussein was afraid of the Shah and his army. My country had never been at war. During the Shah's dynasty, Saddam had tried a few times to show off his power, but the Iranian army forced Iraq's retreat. Now, Saddam dared to attack. Iran seemed like an orphan, vulnerable to any outside force.

I was afraid for my family, my father, mother, and my two sisters. I was even worried for Bijan. What was happening to them? I couldn't think clearly. Life was playing yet another nasty and brutal game.

I looked at my brother and asked, "What will happen to us? I mean, how we can fly back to Iran. I am worried to death about Mom and Dad. I want to be with them, but I don't want to drag my son back into that Islamic hell."

A rush of panic overcame me, and I started to sob. Thousands of thoughts and images were spinning in my head. War was destroying my country, killing families and leveling their homes.

Frightened and injured children were screaming for their mothers. Iraqi soldiers were harassing and humiliating people in Arabic. They were opening fire on innocent people who were dying without knowing the reason.

We tried for several days to contact our family, finally finding my father at home. In his usual way, he sought to sound happy and casual. All he could say was that they were doing fine, that we should not be worried about them.

He mentioned that the war was far from Tehran, but I wondered, for how long. I did not want to let my dad go. I wanted to keep him talking to know he was safe. I was afraid if I let go, I would never be able to see them or to speak with them again. Even in my darkest moments, I had never been this frightened.

But soon the line went dead. When I hung up, I felt as if one of the most precious parts of my life had ended. It would be ten days until I could get through again, this time, to my husband. My son spoke first. I knew James adored and missed his father. His dad was his hero. I only wish Bijan were one.

Bijan told me not to worry that he was safe. There were no flights to Iran; therefore, my return was not an issue. I said I had recently learned I could apply for political asylum because of the situation in Iran. In response, he screamed: "Are you crazy? Did you lose your mind? If you apply for asylum, do you know what the government could do to me?"

I answered, "You can tell them it was my decision, and you didn't know anything about it. It is a great opportunity for James to grow up in Switzerland and go to school here, instead of Islamic-controlled schools in Iran. Think about his future. Don't make the same mistake, again."

He screamed: "What mistake?"

Being a safe distance, I could be honest about how I was feeling and what I was thinking. He couldn't touch me.

I continued, "Don't you remember England? I begged you not to return to Iran after Khomeini had arrived and opened his Islamic butcher shop. You refused to listen and made your son and me pay the consequences. That mistake. I'm talking about living in hell."

Bijan snapped, "Forget about applying for any status that will keep you and my son away from Tehran. You have to bring him back as soon as flights are available. If you don't, the government will hold me responsible for your actions. Do not play with my life."

That was the end of the discussion. When I hung up, James said, "Mama, are we going home? I miss Daddy."

That evening, Edwin and I sat on the balcony, talking about life. I told him that if it were not for our family, I would never go back. With the war and all of its surrounding uncertainty, I wanted to be with them.

Edwin was against my returning. He tried to convince me to stay, saying we could then get the family out of the country. But who could know how long that might take. A couple of weeks later, I bought tickets for one of the first flights scheduled for Tehran.

The flight back was reminiscent of when we left England. I wondered about the mostly Iranian passengers, who they were and why they were returning. Women were covered from head to toe, some wearing chadors, others, like me, had covered their hair with long scarves, legs with jeans, and curves with long coats.

I resented my Islamic dress, the knot of my scarf under my chin was suffocating. But based on Khomeini's fatwah, I had no alternative. Women's hair was considered a distraction to men. A scarf must cover it in the presence of any man, except for one's husband. To me, if a strand of hair could distract them, it must not be a very compelling belief.

As James dozed off, I put the story down I had been reading to him and looked out the window of the plane at the vast and bright blue sky. What awaited me? By some miracle, could my husband have truly missed me and decided to be kind and cherish the life we were sharing? I didn't think so, in fact, I wished I did not have a child with him.

Upon landing, I tightened my scarf, buttoned my mantel, took my son's hand and exited into the unknown. No one was waiting at the airport for us, and no one was home when the cab dropped us off.

Bijan was at the theater and being uncertain about our safety; I had not informed my family of our arrival. It was only the second flight to Tehran since the war had begun, the first had been shot down by the Iraqis.

My son, excited to be back, ran around the house calling for his dad as I collapsed into a chair in the hall, too tired to unpack. I called out to James, "Your dad is at work." He came and jumped on my lap with a smile, so happy and content. Kissing him, I said, "Let's call your grandparents."

First, we spoke with my family; then I called my in-laws. Not long after, a key could be heard unlocking the door. There was my husband, standing in the entrance. Like a bullet, my son shot into his arms. Bijan hugged and kissed him while James was telling him about the zoo we had gone to, the park he played in, and the cartoons he had seen.

At a distance watching them, I suddenly had an overwhelming feeling. A deep sensation, like a profound message to my body and soul, telling me "Something which used to be there, is gone." It was a voice, repeating itself in my head as I looked at Bijan. As he came towards me for a hug and kiss, I was numb to what was happening.

I was still numb when I sat for a cigarette and a cup of coffee after Bijan left to return to the theater for the afternoon performance, saying James could go along and promised to be home as soon as he could. The voice stayed with me.

I kept myself busy unpacking. Then I started to clean the house, which had all the signs that a woman's touch was needed. While I was fixing dinner, Bijan and James came home. As usual, my son talked all about the comedy piece he had seen. He was still talking about it later when I put him in bed and kissed him good night.

The voice in my head persisted through Bijan and I sitting together for a nightcap, with me still trying to understand this feeling that seemed to be here to stay. That night we made love. Bijan was very loving and tender, saying we shouldn't travel alone but be together wherever we go. Even during love-making, my inner voice would not leave me alone.

ಜ⭒ಲ

The next day, James and I visited my family. They opened presents I bought on our trip, and we talked about Iran and the war. All the while, my son sat on my dad's lap. He adored his grandchild. Mom had cooked her usual delicious food. I couldn't imagine life without them. I was happy to be back, despite the odds under the Ayatollah.

While catching them up on Edwin's life and the possibility of our staying in Switzerland with him, my dad said, "Although I never want to be away from my children, it would have been much wiser for you and James to stay in Europe. This country in going through hell and this is just the beginning."

Twenty-Five

I wish I could say life returned to normal. Nothing was normal in my country after the disaster called the Islamic revolution. If that had not been enough, now we were being attacked on our own soil.

Driving was difficult if not impossible at night. No lights were allowed after a certain hour to avoid Iraqi bombs. We had to paint or cover the lights of our cars in navy blue. The city was in complete darkness.

People were hanging black curtains or covering windows with black papers. No one in Iran would have even imagined that our lives would ever be this way. Our heaven had become hell.

Life had become a game of hide and seek. During the day, we had to hide from Khomeini's slaughtering guards, and at nights from Saddam Hussein's bombers. Such was life after the Shah. Arrests and executions occurred daily. The government forced those, who were pardoned by the regime, to join the army and go to war.

People stood in line for hours to buy the basics needed for survival. There was no longer a free market. Those who still had money were the only ones who could afford the inflated prices of what had become of the "open" market.

Since the rise of the Islamic State, a social class of "nouveau riche" - those with ties to the regime - had confiscated mansions, property, farm land, cars, houses, antiques, apart-ments and every other possible possession they could take. The rightful owners had been executed, imprisoned, or if they were lucky, had long ago run away.

Announced in the evening newspaper was a new passport application, declaring those formerly issued by the Pahlavi regime worthless. Anyone wanting a new one had to fill out this new application and send it to the responsible agency.

Deep in my heart, I did not want to believe that my pass-port, bearing the emblem of a lion holding a sword, no longer represented my identity abroad. Others sent in their forms. Bijan and I did not.

The streets were now filled with revolutionary guards, reminding us of the Gestapo. At any given moment something could go wrong. Someone could be arrested or executed on the spot.

Stress was inherent in daily life. While facing this social horror, the domestic one I faced at home continued. Life with my husband was a worsening battle front.

Although I had hoped my trip to Switzerland would open Bijan's eyes and make him appreciate what he had, matters only got worse. He was spending more time away than at home with James and me. After work, it was parties and social gatherings, to which he never invited me.

His excuse was that the crowd was not to my standards, but added it was not my place, admitting it was more about control. I spent most of my time at home with James.

A female neighbor invited me to go horseback riding with her and her daughters. The club asked me to ride with them. It would be good for my son, as well. I was so excited, but let her know I would have to ask Bijan.

Of course, Bijan disagreed, pointing out all sorts of problems that might arise. Was he jealous of horses, too? His reasoning, as usual, was flawed. I explained that we would get a ride with our neighbor and her daughters. I could not understand why he refused. As it was, he was never home to see us. What was the difference?

Finally, he agreed. Now James and I at least had something for which we could be excited. Spending a few hours three times a week riding horses was blissful.

Soon I learned to ride well. From the back of my horse, I could see my son happily riding his. I loved seeing the happiness in his big, shiny, dark brown eyes and hearing his sweet laughter.

However, even those few hours of joy and freedom did not last. One day after training when we returned the horses to their stables, we were told to meet at the main hall. All the trainers and student riders were there. No one knew why.

A few minutes later, a few familiar faces entered, then, to everyone's disbelief, a mullah in a turban appeared, going straight to the podium. Into the microphone, he said: "In the name of God All Mighty, in the name of Imam Khomeini and twelve apostles, today I am here to tell you that women, under no circumstances, are allowed to ride at this facility with the usual riding outfit.

"These clothes are not permitted in Islamic society. We will not tolerate this. Women must wear long dark colored scarves, not riding hats. The riding pants should not be tight and provocative, which is a shame and dishonor to decent Muslim women. Disobedience will be actively punished according to Islamic revolutionary rules and guidance."

He finished, "In the name of All Mighty God and Imam Khomeini."

Without looking in any woman's direction, the mullah left.

My neighbor's face showed utter confusion, still trying to understand what she just heard. I asked jokingly, "What do you think? Should we wear a scarf under the riding hat or put on the hat first, then a scarf on top?"

She smiled bitterly without saying a word.

That was the day I stopped horseback riding lessons.

Life became monotonous, a silent but deadly wheel, turning round and round causing fear and confusion. Bijan's jealousy meant I could only visit my parents and Narine, who by now was married and had a son. Even if I could be more active, there was nothing else to do.

I recalled that in the days before this Islamic Stone Age, whether angry or sad, I could at least stroll in beautiful parks, shop, walk along the streets and be among happy, smiling faces. Now, leaving the house was like stepping into enemy territory. I avoided it as much as possible.

The more I confined myself to the house, the more time my husband spent away from home. He began a habit of not coming home at night. His excuse was the nightly curfew and danger of being arrested, especially, if he had consumed alcohol, which often was the case. The punishment would be eighty-to-one-hundred lashes.

As for me, I cared little about what Bijan did, but his ignorance toward his son who missed him and constantly asked for him, I could not understand. He had wanted a baby so badly, got his wish, and now seemed to have no feelings for his only child.

When Bijan was home, we hardly spoke. There was nothing in common anymore. Between eating and watching TV, we argued and fought. Our sex life was dead, as he would either be gone for the night or, if home, uninterested.

One night, we had a couple who we had met in England, over for dinner with their three-year-old daughter. We talked mostly about our lives under the current political system. Suddenly, out of nowhere in the middle of having a good time, my husband said, "I made a big mistake, I am in trouble and don't know how to free myself."

I tried to grasp what I had heard. My guests and I traded puzzled glances, not knowing what to say. Why was he admitting to some mistake in front of our guests? He stopped there, leaving us to wonder.

The relaxed and friendly atmosphere changed. Bijan had brought up a very private issue with casual friends. Confused and embarrassed, I wanted the get together to be over. It seemed Bijan always tried to shatter my pride. I wondered if I even had that left.

Finally, our guests made an awkward exit, still curious and puzzled. I tucked James into bed and joined my husband, who was seated in the TV room sipping his drink.

I sat next to him and asked, "Talk to me, what is wrong with you? What have you done so wrong, and why did you admit it in front of our guests? Did you become addicted to drugs? Heroin? For God's sake, what are you hiding? What is happening with you?"

He responded, "Nothing is happening, and, no, I am not addicted to anything. Things will get better eventually. It is not that important. Don't worry." Suddenly he was acting so casual as if he had not dropped a bomb at dinner. He took his drink to the bedroom and asked that I join him.

"No, you go ahead," I said, "I have to clean up." Boy, did I! My kitchen and my life.

The next morning, he went to work after breakfast, leaving me with a thousand questions. I knew he would never tell me the truth. I would have to find out for myself.

Bijan began disappearing for days, and I began attending social events and parties alone. I damned the day I said, "I do," but it was too late to dwell on it. I was living in Bijan's house but waiting for the day I could take James and go somewhere he would never find us.

Bijan was still the same animal who would hit me for no reason. Where should I go to complain, who was going to arrest him, the Islamic regime?

I remember one day, one of our Muslim friends told me to read a part in their Qur'an, Chapter 4 Verse 33, where it is written, "As for those (wives) from whom ye fear rebellion, admonish them and banish them to beds apart, and scourge them."

It was a bitter, though not new, realization that Bijan was following his religion. The more he raised his hand to me, the more I hated him.

Amazingly, even his strikes no longer hurt. The more I was subjected to his brutality, the stronger and more committed I would become. I was mentally stronger; he was too weak to break me, and I knew I would leave him. Besides, my son gave me reason to survive, which kept me sane and motivated.

Twenty-Six

Tehran was a beautiful city, the new regime aside. Walking along Pahlavi Avenue, lined with tall Sycamores on both sides, was a great pleasure. The trees formed an arch as their branches met high above the thoroughfare. The rays of the sun filtered through, brightening everything.

Boutiques, fancy coffee shops, fantastic restaurants, and the best discos and cabarets had lined both sides of the bustling street in the days before the revolution. Gradually, many were closed, taken over by extremists, or overrun by guards, lending a sense of oppression to Tehran's longest avenue.

Taking Pahlavi north, one could reach the proud mountains surrounding the city, with their crystal clear rivers meandering through the valley, cooling the scorching summer days by evening time. The breathtaking expanse of nature was a welcome refuge, whether one was feeling happy or down.

Under the Shah, there were many public pools, and many Iranians had their own. By Khomeini's order, based on his Islamic rules, women and teenaged girls were forbidden to swim even at their homes on the chance a male neighbor might observe another man's wife not fully covered, including her hair.

Full coverage was mandatory outside the privacy of her home, regardless of the temperature and even in her backyard.

Should someone knock, she must cover herself before answering, lest it be any man other than her spouse.

One of those summer days, James and I heard such a knock. Thankfully, it was Mahnaz, the girlfriend of my youngest brother-in-law. She often visited, with or without her boyfriend.

Bijan had not come home the previous night, using his usual weak excuses. "You know very well Khomeini's guards are checking every car and passenger in every corner of the city. If I was stopped and found to have been drinking, could you imagine the consequences? I can't risk driving at night."

His tired line was humiliating and an insult to my intelligence.

When Mahnaz asked about my husband, I said, "He's whoring around, probably." The word "probably" belied that somewhere inside, I still did not want to accept his apparent infidelity.

I can still hear her voice: "If I were you, I would have spat on this life and left long ago."

Mahnaz was my confidant. She knew what I was going through; I had opened my heart about the abuse from my husband and the horror of life under Khomeini. She was the only one who knew things I had kept from everyone, including my parents.

Her words were a slap of reality, reminding me of the extent of the humiliation I was allowing. I used to think highly of myself and never underestimated my being. What was wrong with me? Why was I subjecting myself to this? Any other self-respecting woman would have left long ago.

But I had a reason to stay, my son. I knew Bijan would use his child to manipulate the situation. Bijan would never give me full custody, despite his own inability to care for James.

I could never leave my son behind. Bijan had never read him a bedtime story, changed a diaper, spent one sleepless night, taken him to the zoo or the park, been there for doctor appointments, or even been home for any length of time to just be with him.

Bijan had mentioned his previous wife's inability to bear children was his reason for divorce. Having a child was merely proof of his manhood. He had produced a male heir. He need not extend further effort.

Mahnaz and I decided to have lunch at a nearby restaurant. Sitting there, I was aware of the knot of my scarf at my throat. It gave me a choking sensation that I felt with each swallow, but getting to leave the house was worth it. However, the respite would be cut short.

James' food was untouched. He said he wasn't feeling well. It was necessary to return home quickly, where I could put him to bed after some orange juice and aspirin. After a few hours and a worsening fever, I thought it best to get him to the hospital.

There I was assured that, despite the high fever, there was no reason for worry, but was given a prescription, nonetheless. Back at home, my son had no appetite for dinner, so I held him in my arms to watch his favorite cartoons and at least have some soup.

During the night, his fever remained high. I was frightened and wished Bijan was there to help me take care of our son. This sleepless night was the longest of my life, worrying about my child and having no idea where his father was when I needed him most. Finally, the morning arrived with no change.

With no time for self-pity, I grabbed a towel and a bucket that I filled with ice, called a cab, and holding James in my arms, rushed to the children's hospital.

Throughout the unbearably long taxi ride, I rubbed his forehead, legs, hands, face and chest with the cold cloth, one minute begging God for help, the next threatening him with abandonment if he didn't.

This desperate back-and-forth continued, until finally, I pleaded, "Please, God, spare my child. Make him the same healthy boy. If I lose him, I will die."

At the hospital admission desk, the nurse told me there was not a single free bed. That rejection was my last straw. I exploded and demand they admit him, refusing to leave. I started cursing the regime and a hospital that couldn't even receive a possibly gravely ill child.

A man approached and introduced himself as a children's doctor. I recognized the name. He was one of the best and few who had not fled Iran. He mentioned, though not on call, he had just stopped by to finish some paperwork. It was the miracle for which I had begged.

He suggested a test for meningitis, but it meant extracting fluid from my son's spine with a brutally large needle. Seeing it, I collapsed in the corner of the waiting area, my legs unable to support my grief or take me into my son's room, from which I soon heard him scream.

I cried hysterically, knowing I could not help him and feeling as if my sanity had broken. There was no bravery left and not a care about my surroundings or the opinions of on-lookers.

The doctor broke my stupor when he finally approached and convinced me of James' stable condition. They had transferred him to a private room, at which point I called the family. A few hours later, everyone arrived except Bijan.

My sleepless vigil began. As James slept, an IV unit hovering above, I obsessively checked his forehead and face to make sure his temperature didn't rise.

Finally, somewhat settled, my thoughts turned to Bijan. Where in the hell was he? Probably in someone's bed. He did not even know how close we came to losing James. Why think of these things now? I was mentally and physically spent. All that mattered was my child.

The next day, the fever was gone, but hours at a testing facility followed. The prolonged high temperature meant possible brain damage. An excruciating headache had caused James to cry through it all, and my familiar feeling of unbearable helplessness returned.

Back at the hospital, I was trying to get him to eat some soup when Bijan walked in. It had taken him almost two days to realize his son was fighting for his life. Despite this, James was overjoyed to see his dad. Bijan and I had little to say to each other. His indifference hurt as it suddenly sunk in that I had faced this nightmare alone. But this was not the time to think about my problems with Bijan.

Later, the doctor informed us the danger was over. This time, my tears were of joy and relief. I could take my son home. But I also cried for my inner pain. I did not let on to Bijan that I felt degraded.

For the next few days, he lavished our son with toys and gifts and came home after work, spending time with us and playing with James. The child was thrilled; happiness seemed to radiate from his sparkling, big dark eyes. Soon, though, Bijan had returned to spending two-to-three nights away. The sorry excuses returned.

His fears were not unfounded. Actors were considered supporters of the Shah, and the Islamic Regime was against the profession. Khomeini's guards were in every corner, ready to arrest anyone for any reason. But I faced fears, as well, including home invasion, robbery, rape and torture, which had become commonplace. I, too, was living in hell, but that didn't stop me from returning home. Bijan had no excuse to stay away.

Still hoping to escape with James one day, I continued to live the life of a widow.

Twenty-Seven

One day, Bijan informed me that we were going to move to an apartment building where one of his friends and their family lived. It was more secure than our former place.

At first, I didn't want to go. I liked our house, the area, my garden and indoor space where James could play. Then it occurred to me, with all that was happening in the country, perhaps it would be safer in an apartment. I would also have more opportunities to socialize and forget my loneliness.

Not long before, there had been an explosion at a meeting of Islamic revolutionary leaders; seventy-two of them had died. The climate in the city was tense and even more chaotic.

It was thought to have been an inside job. Anarchy ruled. Everyone was in danger, as outlaws ran the country. During this turmoil, Bijan didn't bother to check on his family or even call to see if we were safe.

Two days before we were to be at our new place, all but a few things were packed, thanks to hired movers and Bijan's brothers. Having stayed out the night before, Bijan made a rare appearance after work.

He approached me in the kitchen after dinner, wanting to hug and suggesting we go to bed. His shamelessness floored me; given there clearly was no love between us.

"How daring you are to want to have sex with me," I said. "Your touch would sicken me. Who do..." Without waiting for me to finish, he started walking towards the bedroom. I followed him to the room; I was not done talking. His expression was cold, colder than ice.

He undressed, kicking off his shoes and taking off his pants and shirt. Suddenly, a million volts of electricity went through me, as if hit by lightning. There he stood with his chest and neck covered with hickeys.

I went closer and ran my fingers over the marks as if doing so would make what I saw believable. He just stood there smirking shamelessly, with no trace of panic or guilt. I was disgusted. In my anger I said, "at least have some decency, not to change in front of me. You are like a low life street whore."

Despite knowing just who Bijan's was, his behavior, love for me, our sex life, all had changed for the worse. Once again, I foolishly thought he would not cheat. He used to say, "You are the woman I've always wanted. I am proud to be your husband. I am the luckiest man in the world, to have you at home as my wife and lover, and you are the mother of my child."

Early in our marriage, I had warned him by saying, "If one day you cheat on me, don't bother to come home. I will not accept stupid excuses like, 'Honey, I'm so sorry. I was drunk. It will never happen again.'"

Now facing my dread, could I follow through on my threat? What could I do? The answer was right there, "I should leave." I decided the next day I would pack, tell Bijan I am divorcing him, and move to my parents with my son. They could watch James while I looked for a job.

Of course, acting was out, but surely, I could easily find a job, though prospects might not be great for a woman in Iran.

Maybe we could leave the country, but that meant paying human smugglers, which was extremely risky for a young woman with a small child. Desperate to escape Bijan and the regime, I was ready to try anything, including risking mountain terrain and ocean depths.

I began to cry in sorrow for James. His childhood had turned into a nightmare. During my pregnancy, I read that the first three years of life are crucial for one's future well-being. Bijan had ruined my son's first three years. I would never forgive him.

By morning, my pride still hurt, but not as much as knowing I had failed. I packed a few things and fixed breakfast for James. We were ready to hit the road. Strangely enough, I was happily anticipating what was to come.

Bijan came to the table nonchalantly, but his demeanor changed when he saw I had dressed and packed a bag, which sat in the corner. I kept smiling and joking with James until he decided to play in his room. He said, "Mama, come and play with me."

I said, "Later, sweetheart, later we will play a lot."

Back at the table, Bijan sipped his tea, smoked and looked curiously at me, not knowing what was going on. Strangely calm, I said, "Bijan, I want a divorce. I don't want to live with you any longer."

As if he was not expecting these words, he asked, "What did you say?"

Barely able to look at him, I snapped back, "Can't you hear? I said I want a divorce."

"What else do you want?" he asked, coldly.

I replied, "Nothing but a divorce and my son. Everything else is yours."

"You can't take my son," he said. "If you want a divorce, that's fine, but forget about taking James with you. You will never have custody, and there isn't a thing you can do about it.

All I have to do is tell the Islamic court you are going to raise him as a Christian. It is a battle you won't win.

"Islamic law allows boys to stay with their mothers until five. You are too late. One more thing, even if I die, my parents have more rights to him than you. They can take him from you."

The implications of Sharia Law had not occurred to me. I tried to stay calm and not raise my voice for my son's sake saying, "Why do you even refer to James as your son? Where were you when I had to take him to the hospital? Where were you when he was asking for you and missing you? Good fathers spend time with their kids.

"You know very well you are not a father or husband material. You just use him as a weapon whenever I say I want a divorce. You have gone too far this time. I can't stand you near me."

Bijan was quiet for a change, listening before attacking.

I said one more thing; "Bijan, if you try to take James or go to your mullahs for so-called Islamic justice, I swear to God, I will sleep with every one of those dirty mullahs if that is what it takes to get my child. I am prepared to do anything to keep my son. Trust me, Bijan, you won't win this battle."

His response was an immediate and brutal assault. He grabbed my hair, threw me to the floor, and began punching and kicking, hysterically, "You whore. Go ahead and sleep with them. You won't live to see the day I divorce you and give you my son."

I had become immune to the physical pain. All I could do was cover my face and head and pray that James would not enter the kitchen. I could hear the radio in his room. Luckily, his music was loud enough to muffle the sound.

Bijan finally tired and left the room to shower and dress. It felt as if he had pummeled my bones to powder. Blood ran from my nose down my top. As soon as possible I ran to the bathroom to tend my aching body, not wanting James to see my state.

From behind the door, I heard James say, "Mama, Daddy is taking me out, I will see you later, bye, I love you." Between tears and pain, I managed to say, "Have fun honey, I love you too."

The door shut behind them. I got into the shower and let out all the frustration, pain, humiliation, and isolation in an animalistic cry.

I stayed under the shower for what seemed like hours, trying to wash the misery away, knowing that water was not going to help. Only God could wash away my pain and save me. Finally out of the shower and dressed, I picked up the bag still sitting in the kitchen, and I left.

The reality of being without James for the first time engulfed me during the cab ride to my parents. Finally escaping to go home to my parents was a miracle to rejoice in; doing it without my son was unbearable.

Looking out onto the streets, even pedestrians and people in other cars seemed to share my despair. There was no joy in my life or Tehran.

ಬಲೆ⊃

"Miss, we're here." The driver's voice brought me back to reality.

Mom came to the door, expecting me. Dad, with his kind eyes, was right behind her. He reached for my bag and set it inside the doorway. Wrapping me in one of his soothing hugs, he recited, "You were lost. Now you are found. You were dead. Now you are alive." With a huge sigh, I melted into the safety of my father's arms.

Mom had prepared her usual delicious lunch, and the conversation stayed light, despite the worry in their eyes at James' absence. I was relieved not to have to explain much to my father who was wise enough to grasp this was no short visit. Besides, Mom kept nothing from him.

After the meal, Dad retreated to his room while my mother and I sat in the living room to have some coffee. Even small movements hurt, but I'd become a master at hiding it.

Taking a long drag on my cigarette, I watched the smoke dissipate, just like my carefree youth had faded and finally disappeared in the years since I'd left this house.

The smell of freshly brewed coffee reminded me of the years I had lived in the house. I had never foreseen what would come to be my unhappy present. With feigned calm, Mom moved a tray of fruit and pastries closer to me and sat down.

"Mom, this morning I had a fight with Bijan. I told him I want a divorce."

Surprised, she said, "One fight and you want a divorce?"

If she only knew what I had been through in silence all these years, she would understand why I found this question insulting.

But then, I had never shown her the bruises, never told her of my personal war of mental and physical abuse. Could I tell her though married, I lived as if alone, just trying to survive and raise my son? I could not. Knowing would be of little use now.

I recalled Bijan, crying and saying, "Linda, if you don't marry me, I will die, I will kill myself." Perhaps he meant, "Linda, if you marry me, you will die, I will kill you."

Suddenly, my mother's voice was asking "Why don't you tell me what is happening to you? What is in your heart, child? What are you hiding?"

I just said, "Mom, there is more to it. It is not just one fight. I wouldn't give up for one fight. You know me better than that. If I stay with Bijan, I will lose my identity and even my very existence."

She sipped her coffee nervously. I continued, "Bijan said if I insist on divorcing, he will take James. I can't let that happen. Bijan is not the father my son deserves. Besides, I can't live without my child."

After a long pause, she asked, "So, what do you want to do?"

With a shrug, I said, "I don't know. Maybe I should talk to a lawyer about what options I have, if any, under the Islamic regime. I have to try. There has to be a way out for both of us."

Twenty-Eight

I felt like a bird trapped in a cage, trying to fly, but only hitting cold metal. As evening approached on the first day at my parent's house, I wondered what James was doing at that moment. Was he sleeping? Who had tucked him into bed? Who had read him a story? Was Bijan taking care of him properly? Was he asking where I was?

I began to pray to Mother Mary, asking her to save my son, although she could not save her own when Roman soldiers were crucifying him in front of her horrified eyes. I pleaded. I was not as strong as she was, I was just a sinner.

The door to my room opened to my mother's silhouette. As she stepped in, I felt the weight of the trouble I had caused her since I had learned to walk and talk.

She hugged me silently, putting my head on her chest, kissing and caressing my hair. In her heavenly loving arms, I began to sob. The pain, suffering, sleepless nights, wounds, humiliation, and insults erupted like a volcano.

In her arms, I didn't have to pretend to be strong. I exhausted myself from crying, fell asleep and didn't wake up until dawn. Then I sat for a long time wondering once again if my son was receiving proper care. In my rush to escape, I forgot to grab a piece of his clothing to have his scent to bring him closer. No one smelled the same.

An hour later, I heard my mother calling me to breakfast. Getting out of bed, my body felt like it had been run over by a semi. The adrenalin from the day before was gone, and a sharp pain went through my bones.

The persona of happiness I wore to hide my emotions throughout my years with Bijan was hard to maintain in front of my parents. But I didn't want them to know things that would cause them more pain and anger. I had already caused enough anguish.

During breakfast, we all acted normally, but I noticed anxious looks between my parents. I didn't know what to say to comfort them. After breakfast, my father left for work. I wanted to lie down, but I mentioned to my mom that maybe we could have a cup-reading ceremony when I got up.

This traditional Armenian custom involved slowly enjoying a small cup of very thick coffee until the grounds gathered at the bottom of the empty cup. Then the saucer would be placed upside down on the top of the cup, and both would be quickly turned. This way, the thick coffee grounds would slide toward the cup rim and into the plate, leaving trails and shapes to be interpreted after the cup was once again, turned right-side up.

Usually, they would translate into hopeful words or future happenings. I didn't place much stock in the predictions but found the ritual social and fun, except once, years before, when I was still living with my parents, acting in movies and dating Bijan without my parent's knowledge.

One sweltering summer afternoon, I noticed an elderly woman knocking on our neighbor's door. Apparently, no one was home. Feeling sorry for her in the heat, I invited her in for some water. She happily agreed and followed me in. When I handed her the water, she said, "You've been kind, go make coffee, and I will read your cup."

Meanwhile, Mom and Narine returned from shopping. I told my mom of the request and headed to the kitchen to prepare coffee. Returning with four cups and some fresh summer fruit, I found the old woman and my mother already engaged in conversation. Soon we had reached the bottom of our coffee cups, and she began reading. Mine was last.

Studying it carefully, she began, "You travel a lot for your job." True enough. Acting took me to different places. She added, "There is a man in your life. He has a mark on his face; it could be mustache, beard, or a mole." Again, she was right, Bijan had a mustache. I grew uncomfortable as Mom became increasingly attentive to the revelations.

The lady went on, "This man in your life, doesn't share your religious beliefs." At that point, I felt like throwing the cup out the window. From where did this come? Could it be that our neighbor had told her about me and my profession? But they hadn't known about my relationship with Bijan.

What had been a harmless social activity was becoming risky for me. No one had ever hit this close to my private life. My mother's look of disbelief and anger made me question my kindness to a stranger.

When our guest left, I sat, shell-shocked. I had never believed in coffee cup readers, yet this woman brought my secret life into the daylight. Alone with me now, Mom asked, "Linda, what was that all about in your cup?"

I thought to myself, "Quick, Linda, come up with something."

I said, "Mom, since when do you believe in cup readings? There is no man in my life. Only one thing she said was right, I travel."

Mom shrugged and dropped it. I was relieved and have been uninterested in coffee cup rituals ever since.

I took a painkiller and went to lie down. It was eight in the morning. I lay there wondering, "How is James? Did he have breakfast already? How was his night without his mother?" I couldn't keep thoughts of him out of my mind or my brain from obsessing about getting us both out of Bijan's life. I wanted to sleep and wake to it being over.

But I couldn't even stay in bed. My brain went in circles, desperately trying to find a solution, a way out of Bijan's life. I had always disliked people who felt sorry for themselves, surrendering to destiny without a fight. But now, I was becoming one of them.

I joined my mother in the kitchen, where she was preparing lunch. Sitting down, I studied my mom's face, thinking about her life path. She was still beautiful. I asked, "Mom, could you please just hug me, I feel lost."

She sat and motioned me to sit on her lap. Despite that I was in my late twenties, I sat on her lap like a two-year-old. Out of nowhere, she said, "No one knows how I regretted my trip to Armenia those years ago. If I had not gone, this would never have happened.

"You would not have married Bijan, who is the reason for our family's misery. Your father wanted to call him last night and confront him about what he has been doing to you and why you've lost so much weight. He used to think that difficulty taking care of your son was the cause, now he knows better. I stopped him because of his heart condition. He hardly slept."

That is when I realized coming home had not been the right decision. I had no right to bring my problems to my parents; they had suffered enough.

Standing up, I said, "Mom, I need to go out for a walk. I'll be back soon." Without waiting for her reaction, I covered myself and left.

Walking aimlessly in the familiar neighborhood, I noticed all the women looked alike, all covered from head to toe, with their kids next to them and husbands walking a few steps ahead.

A few blocks away, I heard a voice behind me, "Hey, monkey!" I kept walking. The voice came closer.

"I'm talking to you, monkey." Looking back, I saw two of Khomeini's guards, one in his thirties, the other, who was taunting me, a mere teenager.

"Did your stupid mother teach you to talk this way?" I snapped. "You are the monkey, you idiot. Get the hell out of my sight before I slap your stupid, ugly face." As if they were not expecting my outburst, I saw their hands go to their waists, pulling out guns.

The younger came closer, shouting, "I can kill you right here. You have insulted Islam and us. You dare to talk back. Why aren't you properly covered? Why is your neck bare?"

Somehow, I felt no fear of them or their guns. Meanwhile, a jeep drove close and stopped. Inside were three other guards whose faces made me want to throw up.

The shouting continued, "Who the hell do you think you are? What was your mama doing before the revolution, serving her clients in the 5th District?" The 5th District was known to be the red milieu, where whores lived and worked.

The Jeep door opened. In a second I was surrounded by all of them. The one that looked to be the boss came toward me and began pushing me toward the jeep.

I knew the consequences of being arrested by these mercenaries. I would disappear forever. I had heard many horror stories of people gone with no trace. Getting into that jeep meant stepping into oblivion. But how could I fight five men?

Meanwhile, people began to gather and dared to defend me. "What do you want from her? Why don't you leave her alone? Her cover is proper." An old woman approached the guards, begging them to release me. It had become a huge scene.

The apparent leader approached me. Without looking in my eyes, he said, "Today is your lucky day, go home woman." Before they left, the thug who called me "monkey" approached, pointing his dirty finger in my face, saying, "The next time I see you, I will empty six bullets into your monkey head." I looked straight into his eyes and said, "The monkey is the one who brought you to this world."

I was beyond caring if they emptied their guns into my head. Enough of taking crap from men, in particular, these men. I would have liked to have taken their guns and shot them on the spot. Indeed, my hate was stronger than my fear, thus my resistance. My husband could have been one of these guards; he had the perfect character for it.

To everyone's disbelief, the gang jumped in the jeep and left, leaving me and everyone who had come to my aid, alive. At that moment, the elderly woman came close, holding my hand kindly, she said, "Child, you should be careful! Today God was with you, but you should learn to bite your tongue. They could have killed you. Do you want to die? Have mercy on your parents. Promise me you will be cautious. You can't change them or anything else with argument. Go home and be safe."

Twenty-Nine

My numb brain was incapable of rational thought. I was tired of the constant fighting, inside and outside my home. On autopilot, I returned to the safety of my parent's place around noon.

My mother rushed toward me with a hug, saying, "Where were you? We were just about to come and look for you in the streets." She was kissing me like crazy. I said, "Why so much worry mom? I told you I was going for a walk. I lost track of time." I left out that I had almost lost my life.

"Mom, is there any news from James? Did he call?" I asked. Her sad eyes answered, no. I told her how terribly I was missing my son. His face was the first thing I saw each day and the last thing each evening.

As I went to lie down, the shock of being bullied by the guards hit me; how easily one could die in this country. Between the regime and Bijan, my only choice was to find a new home, far from Iran.

I could hear my mother answering the phone. When she called my name, I knew it was James. His sweet voice reminded me of my reason to fight on. He asked, "Mama, where are you? When are you coming home?"

I said, "Soon, Baby, very soon I will be with you. How are you, Sweetheart? Are you ok? Where is your dad? Is he with you?"

My son replied, "Mama, come and see all the toys Dad bought for me. I have a red car I can drive."

"That's great!" I said. "I am so happy for you. But, tell me, have you had lunch?"

"Not yet," he said. "We are going to Grandma's for lunch. Can you come, too?"

All I could say was, "No, Honey, I can't go. I'm with your other grandparents."

He immediately replied, "Let me talk to Grandma! Then I want to tell Grandpa about my car."

I passed the receiver to Mom and went to the kitchen. Hearing James' voice intensified my sense of overwhelming separation. I wanted to fly to him, hold him in my arms, and never let go. Being a mother was more sacrifice than I could bear. Soon Mom was passing the phone back to me.

"Mama, will you read me the story about the baby bears tonight?"

Tears streamed down my face as my heart broke for my innocent child. I said, "I can't tonight, but I will read it later. We can even buy more books for you, Sweetie Pie."

He yelled, "No, Mama! Come home! Don't you love me anymore?"

Pulling together all my strength, I said, "Honey, I love you more than anything in this world. You are a very brave and good boy. I will never stop loving you. Now go play, and I will see you soon. I love you. Be a good boy. Bye, Honey."

Hanging up the phone, I was left to look at my mother. It amazed me to think we were now both mothers, but with very different husbands. She had hit the jackpot when she married my father, who kept her on a pedestal. My gamble had ended up in mayhem and heartache. Now my child was forced to share in the pain.

"Linda, we need to talk," Mom said, motioning for me to sit. "What are you going to do? You can't leave your son without a mother. He needs you, regardless of how you feel. It's your responsibility to take care of him.

"James told me that he thinks he's done something to make you leave and is having trouble sleeping because of scary dreams. On top of that, they've moved, once again. Everything is new and strange. He thinks you don't love him. Linda, this could scar him forever."

Returning home meant surrendering to Bijan. He would know I stayed to be with my son and would never cease using him against me. I wondered how he could insist, knowing I am without love or desire for him.

Swallowing what little pride remained, I packed my bag, kissed Mom goodbye, and headed home, if I could call it that. Only my love for my son gave me the strength to return to Bijan, let alone live under the same roof and sleep in the same bed. In the middle of the hell that awaited me, there was a little angel needing my care.

Thirty

When I got to the house, I had a panic attack. The struggle to breathe made it seem like the air was lacking oxygen. I soon doubted the decision to return. But how could I have stayed at my parents? If only James had been with me, Bijan would not have seen even my shadow again.

Then I saw my son playing in the yard. As I stepped closer, he saw me and ran open-armed to hug me. With him in my arms, I knew why I had returned and soon forgot the rest of the world, including Bijan's treatment of me and the way the guards had harassed me. The horror faded in the love I was feeling for my child.

Kissing and smelling James was as if breathing life into my tired body. He didn't let go of my hand as we went four floors on the elevator as if afraid I might leave him again. I hoped Bijan wasn't home. I didn't want to see him. When we got to the door, he opened it with a grin, moving in for a hug.

What a shameless lowlife. When he saw my cold look, he stepped back, took my bag and went inside, holding the door open for me. Welcome back to hell, I thought. Once inside, I could see he had decorated nicely. He had everything organized, and there were fresh cut flowers on a little table next to the entrance.

I went to the kitchen with James following me, still holding my hand. I sat down, holding him and inspecting every inch of his little body. Suddenly, I saw a large wound next to his ankle that apparently no one had cleaned or treated.

Trying hard to stay calm, I couldn't help but think the worst. I got supplies from the bathroom, cleaned and wrapped the wound, and asked him, "When did this happen? How did you get injured?"

He said, "Yesterday I fell riding my bike."

Relieved, I told him, "You are such a brave boy. I am so proud of you, Sweetheart. Do you feel better now?"

He smiled, kissed my cheek and asked if I would read him a story that night. Of course, I would read whatever he wanted. Delighted, he ran from the kitchen. I stayed, not knowing what to do or what to feel. I didn't want to face or talk with Bijan. There was nothing left to say.

"Linda," I heard Bijan call.

"I'm in the kitchen," I replied.

A few second later, he appeared, standing at the kitchen door, looking at me tenderly. But I was tired of his games.

Sitting down, he said, "You know. Our son isn't the only one who missed you, Bella," What, he was using Italian now? He was probably screwing one.

I said, "Who else, our neighbors?"

He didn't like my reply. I didn't care.

"No, I missed you most of all. It was hard to accept that you were gone. I was lonely and couldn't think about life without you. Everything felt meaningless and empty. I didn't know what to do. Linda, I love you very much.

"You are my wife. I know I haven't been the best husband, I've made many mistakes and I've hurt you. Please forgive me. Give me a second chance to prove I am worthy of your love. Please, Linda, look at me when I am talking to you. Can't you find forgiveness in your heart?"

I turned looking straight into his eyes. I said, "Some months ago, I was reading the story of Pinocchio to our son, where each time Pinocchio lied, his nose grew longer and longer. If that were possible, your nose would be two blocks long and growing."

Bijan looked at me in disbelief. I continued, "You are much older than I am. You should have known this marriage was wrong. You did everything in your power to marry me. Why? Why did you want to marry me so badly?

"I am sure you can find a woman who will make you happy and to whom you will want to be faithful. Go find her. Who knows, maybe one day I will find a man who will make me happy too; unless I've found and lost him already." Out of nowhere, Bernard came to my mind.

Bijan said, "Linda, I would do anything to prove that I've changed. I have learned my lesson. I love you more than you will ever know. Here, I have something for you."

He put a small box on the table. "Open it. You will love it. It's a beautiful set of diamond baguette rings." Noticing that I didn't move, he took the box, opened it and put it in front of me. There were three diamond rings inside, one a wedding band, baguettes all around. The two others were beautifully cut, very delicate and gorgeous. I had never seen rings that beautiful.

I wondered, "Is this the cost of my pride or my love?" I pushed the box back to him, stood up, and walked out of the kitchen.

I went to the bedroom to unpack my bag, wondering whether I should keep it packed. Bijan followed me and placed the box on the table next to the bed. Then he came closer, wanting to hug and kiss me.

Luckily, James came in at that very moment. He was a God-send with perfect timing. Bijan backed away, telling him, "I told you your mom would come home soon. Happy now?" My son smiled at him, then sat on the bed next to me, holding me tightly.

The weeks passed by like the wind, reminding me of lost time and life. Meanwhile, I got to know our neighbors. On the first floor, there was a family of three, just like Bijan and me; they had one son, almost the same age as James.

A friend of Bijan's and his wife who had a son from her previous marriage lived on the second floor. Just below us was a middle-aged couple, with no children.

My first-floor neighbor, Mahtab, was almost my age. She had worked at Foreign Ministry during the Shah's reign and still did, only now under Islamic cover with no makeup.

Being the only Christian in the building, I felt far from my people and friends, who would gather at Church on holy days, light candles and pray in the little chapel.

Karl Marx said religion was "the opium of the people." I had never believed it. My religion kept me alert and strong, closer to God, where I wanted to be. What is a human without belief, without God?

During my childhood, my father read storybooks to us, giving me visions of faraway lands. He also read passages from the Bible, told stories about Jesus, and described the Armenian genocide.

These stories took over my body and soul, my very existence as if mixing with my blood and altering my DNA. By marrying a Muslim, I had lost my connection to my people, but my connection to my faith, beliefs, and God was unbreakable.

Once a week, we would get together to play rummy with our neighbors. I looked forward to it, although it was gambling and anti-Islamic. We were in the safety of our homes, which was better than taking the risk of going out and being stopped at every checkpoint by hostile guards.

On our street, also lived other movie actors and their families. Their parties were a chance to reminisce. The regime had forbidden alcohol throughout the country. A standard joke was, "The Shah taught us to drink alcohol, Khomeini taught us to make it." People were making their own in their homes like amateur chemists.

Since my return, Bijan had been behaving like every other decent husband. But I had seen that before, and it never lasted. At least he was still working at the theater and earning enough money.

Soon it was time to enroll James in his first year of school. We chose Razi School, a French managed school which was close to home, where he could learn to speak French and learn about French culture, along with the usual curriculum.

On the first day, however, despite my son's excitement, I saw little of a French atmosphere as we walked through the gate, across the vast playground, and into the building.

Female teachers were covered head to toe, and the males had beards. Not one wore a suit and tie. It felt the same as encountering those guards on the street. I had to wonder what their education levels were and what my son would learn from them. I wanted to take him and leave, but that was not possible.

A short while later, James told us he had to learn how to pray.

I said, "But, Honey, you already know how to pray. The way you and I do every night, kneeling next to your bed, remember?"

He replied, "No, Mama, I have to learn the way Muslims do, just like my Grandma and Grandpa, when to bend, and when to stand up and what to say, but it's all in a language I don't understand," he said, adding "I have to do it five times a day."

I wanted James to get an education, learn English and French. Now we would have to exchange French for Arabic for the purpose of reciting the Quran.

Bijan noticed my desperation from the living room, where he was having tea and said, "Don't worry. I will teach him our prayers."

I said, "Those prayers are not in Farsi. Now he has to learn Arabic and how to bend over with his ass in the air." Bijan was laughing, saying "Karma is here to get you, Linda."

I said, "This is not karma; this is a curse."

In the evening when our son was practicing the Islamic prayers with Bijan, it was my turn to laugh. James was unable to pronounce Arabic and fell when he tried to put his forehead on the little prayer stone.

Though I was laughing, deep down, I worried for my child. Maybe a word with the school principal would help to change the requirement for James to pray.

The regime and their schools were indoctrinating the young to a radical culture and grooming the young for war. They had been bribing Muslim families with TVs, refrigerators, cars, and cash, to send their boys to the front, where minefields awaited them.

Each soldier wore a plastic key, made in Taiwan, on a chain around their neck. The Regime claimed these were keys to heaven and the martyred would go straight there, where angels were waiting for them.

I had to save my son.

Thirty-One

One night, when we were dinner guests at a movie director's house, the conversation turned to the topic of how to get
out of Iran. Our host mentioned that when the Regime had
published the form for obtaining an Islamic – approved
passport, some people submitted multiple forms for approval.
Now they were selling them. He even knew a man who had
extra forms.

Curious, I asked, "That's interesting. But how is it possible?
Isn't the person's name on the form?"

He answered, "Yes, it is. This is a risky move. But some people are willing to take it."

Still curious, I wanted clarification. "So, if John Doe is on
the form, how could a Jane Doe get a passport with it? Before
he answered, I asked, "How much does he want for a form?"

The price was as high as the risk. I didn't ask any more questions, but the subject intrigued me, despite the danger. It was
mind-blowing to think of the chances people were taking. But
I, too, would do anything to leave.

Later, at home, with James asleep, Bijan and I were watching TV when I asked what he thought about the idea of
applying for passports using one of the illegal forms.

He had no interest, saying, "Do you know what will happen
if they realize the form doesn't belong to the person submitting
it? Long years in prison. It is a terrible idea to pay that much

for something that has not even a one percent chance. That is worse than a gamble; it's suicide."

In bed that night, the thought lingered. Buying the form was the only way to get a passport and leave the country. But the process didn't make sense. It seemed impossible unless a blind person was behind the passport desk. And of course, the seller wouldn't bear any responsibility. It was a lose, lose situation.

At breakfast the next morning, I persisted, asking, "Bijan would you buy a passport form for me?"

He said to me with disbelief, "Are you joking?"

Shaking my head, I replied, "No, I am serious because that is the only way to . . ."

He didn't let me finish, snapping back with "Why do you think that is the only way? There is no way. When they compare your identification to the form, you will be arrested and end up in Evin Prison."

Evin was the most treacherous jail of the era. It was a godless place, and anyone who ended up there would likely never get out, alive, anyway.

"Bijan, I want to try it. If you don't pay, then I'll find a job and pay it myself, or I will ask my father."

"The money is not the issue, Linda," he said. "Why don't you understand? What if you get arrested? What about our family, our son? What will I tell him when they arrest you? 'Mommy is in prison.' Please be realistic and forget about that crazy offer. It will only bring disaster."

I was desperate for a passport, and asked again, "Please, will you give me the money?"

Bijan grew angry, but to my surprise, he said yes. "You can have the damn money, but don't expect me to come to find you when you are in trouble."

With a sigh of relief, I promised not to ask for anything else.

The very next day, I asked Bijan to contact the director and arrange to get a form. Bijan knew I wouldn't give up on the idea. I was happy, excited, and terribly scared. It was a risk I had to take, though. If it worked, freedom would be within reach.

Finally, we met the seller, paid him, and the form was in my hands. All I had to do was submit it and wait for a response from the passport office.

Most of our friends had already left the country. Human smuggling was big business. And the Regime continued to make the lives of people like us, a living hell.

One weekend evening, after spending the day with Bijan's parents, I was helping James with his homework as Bijan sat watching the news when the phone rang.

It was the panicked voice of the wife of an actor who lived near to us. She could hardly breathe. The first thing that came to my mind was that the guards had arrested him.

She immediately said, "Linda, quick clean up your home, Khomeini's guards were here and searched our house, and now they are headed to your place."

I didn't waste a second. I dropped the phone, told Bijan what was happening, and began collecting anything that could give them a reason to arrest us, which meant confiscating all of our belongings and financial assets.

As usual, Bijan froze from panic as I ran around the apartment grabbing anything so-called anti-Islamic, including every video cassette, playing cards, bottles of alcohol, the backgammon board, and pictures from the walls. Thank goodness we were on the top floor, as I was able to hide the bag on the roof.

Bijan urged me to wear my scarf. I objected, saying, "I'm in my home. I don't have to hide my hair from you."

He begged, "Linda, please don't argue with me now. Just do it for our sakes, do it for James."

Feeling his terror, I covered my hair. Not a minute later came banging, and someone shouting, "Open the door!" I rushed to answer, telling Bijan to sit down and let me handle the situation.

To my horror in barged four of Khomeini's guards, pushing me aside and scattering to ransack our home. Covering my hair had been smart. I saw them notice. As if invading enemy territory, they went through every room, closet, drawer, and search behind paintings and under every rug.

I followed one into my bedroom and protested as he went to open a drawer. I snapped, "Those are my undergarments and panties. Are you going to touch or look at the underwear of another man's wife?"

He froze as if hit by the lightening, before leaving the room.

Two of them were going through my kitchen cabinets, opening the fridge, checking everything. There was a bottle of whiskey filled with water. The guard opened it, then upon smelling it, realized it was water, and put it back.

Finally, they gathered in the living room, pulling up chairs to speak with Bijan. They ignored me since I was a woman. Bijan asked if we could offer them anything.

I thought to myself, "I can offer them bullets in their fucking empty heads.

One of them replied, "Yes, a glass of water would be good."

James had come out of his room because of the commotion during their search and was running around like a maniac. I went to comfort him before bringing water to the table. He was pale, and I could see his heartbeat through his t-shirt. While in my arms, he said, "Mama, my heart is jumping. I can't breathe."

I could only say, "Don't worry Honey, everything is all right, mama is here."

I could have exploded but knew I had to control myself. In the kitchen, I found the Scotch bottle containing water. Placing it on a tray with glasses, I delivered it to the coffee table in the living room.

The look on Bijan's face was priceless. He didn't know, if I could, I would have poisoned that water.

Finally, they left. I called to thank our friend for the warning, which likely saved our lives.

A few days after this enemy attack, Ladan, one of my neighbors, asked if I would like to go shopping with her and her daughter. I agreed, taking my son along.

In Vanak Square an elderly woman jumped in front of our car, cursing at us. Ladan nearly hit her. Neither of us understood what would have caused her to lash out at us and almost cause an accident.

Ladan stopped the car, shaking. The woman was fully covered in her chador, still cursing, in vulgar terms in front of the children. Ladan and I stepped out of the car and approached her. She would not stop swearing.

"What is your problem? Have you lost your mind? Why did you jump out like that? Do you want to die? Why are you cursing? Can't you see there are children in the car?"

She shouted, "Whores like you two are my problem. It wasn't enough to be whores at damn Shah's palace. Now you're driving like you own everything. Where are your chadors, you whores?"

I couldn't take it anymore. I stepped closer to this lunatic, while people gathered around. When close enough, I raised my hand toward her chador, saying, "Let me check under your chador. I am sure you are naked underneath, looking for a customer. Be happy you are old. Otherwise, I would beat the crap out of you."

Meanwhile, Ladan shouted, "I should have let you end up under my car, which would have been the end of your miserable life."

The woman backed off and disappeared into the crowd. Ladan and I looked at each other in disbelief. The smallest pleasure so easily could turn to chaos. What do they want from us? How are we going to survive these crazy mobs?

Back in the car, Ladan burst into hysterical crying; this prompted her daughter and James to cry along with her. I, too, joined the bitter chorus with the most anguished melody anyone had ever heard.

Ladan was scared, yet, fuming. She said, "Linda, throughout my life, I have never been insulted to this extent. That woman would have killed us if she had a gun. Did you see the hate in her eyes? What is happening to us? What has happened to kindness and caring for one another?"

There was nothing I could say.

We drove back home, no longer in the mood to spend a casual, fun day with our kids. Living a decent human life was a thing of the past. Even the idea of a simple shopping trip had become far-fetched.

Thirty-Two

The days passed with Bijan once again working long hours and spending almost every day in rehearsal. His new play, ironically, was called "Life is a Bitter Story." His earnings had hit the roof, so money was never an issue. It seemed to be pouring from the sky. He also had resumed coming home drunk.

Meanwhile, I devoted myself to James, whom it seemed, Bijan hardly knew. I would take my son to school, pick him up, and help him with schoolwork.

In times of hurt and desperation, I occasionally thought about cheating on Bijan when fathers who had come to pick up their children after school would flirt and even dare to ask me out.

Their behavior seemed outrageous given they knew I was married, and they were, too. But stroking their egos would not have been worth it, even to get back at Bijan. There was too much potential to hurt James with such a reckless action. I would not risk that.

One night at home, after dining with our downstairs neighbors, Bijan and I ended up fighting over my having visited a friend, who lived with an Argentinean guitar player. The band performed at nightclubs in Tehran.

He jumped at me, throwing me to the floor. I stood and ran for the bedroom. Before I could lock the door, he pushed his way in and chased me to the bed, where he grabbed the top of my head and yanked my hair with all his strength. Agonizing pain hit me as I saw his fist clutching a clump of hair so tightly his veins protruded from his hand.

He was attaching me like a sworn enemy; no mercy, as if only my dead body would satisfy his maniacal and sadistic appetite. As usual, I held back my screaming to spare James the trauma of another fight.

Each violent episode was getting more perilous. I didn't understand how Bijan could function normally in society, and then turn into an animal at home. Would I survive his brutal hands?

With no position or rights as a woman under Islamic laws, I knew I needed a lawyer's advice. I needed to understand if I had any chance of divorcing this madman I was married to and getting sole custody of my son. Soon, a friend referred her uncle, and I took the first available appointment.

With my son in school and Bijan at the theater, I hid under a huge scarf and dark sun glasses and headed to the lawyer's office. It occurred to me that, for the first time, the scarf had a purpose.

When I arrived, the lawyer greeted me with a handshake, which was against Islamic rules. Our hands were not supposed to touch. He appeared to be in his late fifties, professionally dressed with neatly combed salt and pepper hair, he also wore glasses.

I sat in front of his cluttered desk, where he had stacked folders on either side of a thick law book that he apparently had been reading before I got there.

Family pictures in Iranian hand-crafted frames decorated his office, as did popular miniatures and, of course, a portrait of Khomeini's frightening stare.

I knew this poor man had to have that in place or officials would have dangerous suspicions. Khomeini's image saturated the country. One could not escape his evil eyes.

The attorney offered tea, and I politely declined, asking if we could talk about the case.

"Why in such a hurry?" he asked.

I replied, "I have waited beyond that of which I thought myself capable. It's a matter of life and death."

I went on to narrate nine torturous years of my loveless and perilous life since stepping into Bijan's house.

Once I finished, I took a long breath and leaned back in the chair. He didn't speak for a long time. Then, clearing his throat, he said, "I've practiced law in this country for almost two decades. I have never heard of a case this brutal. But, unfortunately, you are out of luck.

"We live in an Islamic-ruled country now. Your son is too old for a mother's custody; you have no place of your own, and no income. Your only option is to move into your parent's home with your child.

It also doesn't help that you are Christian and were once an actor. I am sorry to be so direct, but you do not stand a chance."

I felt helpless. My eyes filled with tears, I asked, "You mean your thick law book has not one page that gives me some right to protection?

He just shook his head and asked, "Do you have a Plan B?"

Back on the sidewalk, I felt a bitter taste like poison. Needing air and time to think, I began to walk. Having a Plan B had never occurred to me. My only plan was to leave the country with James, with or without a passport.

I finally arrived home with no idea how long I'd been gone as if hypnotized to function on autopilot.

"Where were you?" Bijan yelled. Startled, I jumped back to awareness, my hand over my heart.

"What is wrong with you? I almost had a heart attack." I said.

He ignored my comment.

"I asked you a question," he insisted.

Brazenly, I almost told the truth. But I wasn't willing to pay the torturous price if I even gave Bijan a clue I'd been to a divorce attorney.

I came up with a story instead, telling him I had seen a beautiful dress the other day and went back to buy it but, no luck, it was gone. Luckily, he fell for it or was too preoccupied to fight. His thoughts were elsewhere.

So were mine. I had heard nothing of my passport application. Leaving the country illegally via human smugglers seemed to be the only way out. But I wasn't sure I could subject James to such danger. I had heard too many tragic tales of those young and old, losing their lives on that perilous journey.

Later that night, during my normal conversation with God, my prayers turned to asking a certain favor of him.

"Father in heaven, I need your help. Please, make my husband fall in love with another. Then I'll be free, and he will be more willing to let me take his son. I don't know what I have done to deserve this life, but please forgive me, and please answer my prayer."

Life continued its seemingly unfair course until one unforgettable morning when the mailman delivered a strange envelope. Inside, was a passport appointment notice from immigration, requiring that I bring my birth certificate and the original form printed so long ago in the evening paper.

In two months, I would have my passport.

I kissed the letter and held it as if it were treasure. I had not felt such elation since before my marriage. My wish, my dream, was just a few steps away. My soul was joyful.

But fear and panic replaced my joy almost immediately. The risk was real. If authorities found it was not my form, the consequence was prison. The image of my arrest, being hand-cuffed and taken away, played in my mind like one of my former movies.

But the horrifying stories out of Evin prison were worse than any movie. It would be a Twilight Zone of no return after a kangaroo court sentenced me to life imprisonment.

I would be raped, beaten, and tortured, constantly wishing for my inevitable death. What would happen to my son? My parents would both have heart attacks. Perhaps the risk was too great.

At a crossroads, my choice was one prison or another. Each road scared me to death. It was between Bijan or the Islamic State. The latter seemed not that much worse. Only a passport could free me. I would leave the country and build a life my way, where James wouldn't witness his mother's abuse.

I needed a solid plan. But, how could I devise one without knowledge of the building's layout, the level of security, or even the procedure itself? I felt like a blind soldier off to war.

Meanwhile, the days kept counting down, and I remained engulfed in my so-called life. At least James was doing great in school, and Bijan was hardly home. His "overnights" had returned in force. Rarely did we sleep together and barely exchanged a word.

One dreary morning, busy with chores, I gathered clothes to take to the cleaners. Checking pockets, I found some change and a receipt. It was from a jewelry shop for a diamond band.

The description of which matched none of my rings. It was dated a month prior.

I sat on the edge of the bed, holding the receipt in my hand, reading it over and over. Was this piece of paper the answer to my prayer? I sensed my life was about to change for the good.

Still, contradicting emotions flooded me, from the anticipation of freedom to anger, disrespect, and betrayal. I felt my bruised ego. Wasn't I passed that already? Surely, I was not feeling jealous or any remnant of love. I had never felt safe, protected or loved in our relationship.

For all these years, all Bijan did was try to break me, mold me to something like a robot that would carry out any command. But, he didn't know that the more he pushed me into slavery, the more resistant I would become and the more I would fight. Didn't he know he couldn't break me?

The receipt and the possibility of another woman should have been devastating, but aside from a loss of pride, my heart was spared anguish, perhaps because it was now empty.

It then became apparent that God was answering my prayer. He had listened, He was watching me. I wondered when he saw Bijan attacking and brutally beating me, did He cry?

I stood, not knowing what to do next. Despite my wish unfolding, I was weary from the blow I had suffered. In the distance, a phone rang. Suddenly, I realized it was mine.

Thirty-Three

I had no idea how long the phone had been ringing. It was Ladan.

"Hi, Linda! What's up? 'Time for coffee and a chat, maybe?"

I told her I was on my way to the dry cleaners and then had more chores before needing to pick up James. She insisted on joining me.

"I have some dry cleaning myself. We can go together. Besides, I have something important to tell you. I'll be there in 15 minutes." She hung up before I could invent another excuse.

As if officially declaring war, I taped the receipt to the vanity table mirror so Bijan wouldn't miss it.

Ladan arrived with a tray of cookies; she loved Armenian sweets and pastries.

"Here, I brought a Julio Iglesias' cassette. Let's forget about the assholes and listen to his sexy, soothing voice while we enjoy ourselves."

Her behavior seemed out of character. Jokingly, I asked, "Since when do you listen to Julio while drinking coffee and possibly dreaming of Madrid or Barcelona?"

She ignored the friendly jab and started the music.

Ladan appeared rushed and nervous, quickly drinking her coffee and setting her cookie down after one bite. She began:

"Linda, I don't know how or where to start. I feel like throwing up. But there is something you have to know."

With a deep breath and a pause, she continued, "Bijan told my husband he has taken another wife as a Sigheh wife. In Islam, men can recite some lines from the Quran and wed a woman, not legally, but based on Sharia Law. So they cover whoring around with the dress of religion.

"In short, a man can screw as many women as he wants as long as he has recited the magic words. He now feels trapped and doesn't know how to get out."

There was another pause, this time with a pained look, directly into my eyes. Without replying, I took her hand and asked that she follow me to the bedroom. I am sure she expected a breakdown, but instead, I gave her the receipt, saying, "Read this. I found it an hour ago in Bijan's pocket."

Staring at it, she said, "I can't believe this." She had come to comfort me. Instead, I found myself cheering her. "Ladan, I never intended to complain to you or any of my neighbors."

Abruptly, she said, "Linda, we aren't blind. We saw what was going on. We knew you were staying for your son. I don't want to hurt you, but your husband is a *khar* (donkey)!" Calling someone a "donkey" is a big insult in the Iranian culture. Ladan had clearly done her best to insult Bijan.

I said, "I'm not offended or hurt at all. Honestly, I could deal with a donkey, but a whore monger is something else. That is beyond my abilities."

"My blood is boiling," she said. "How can you tolerate this? If it were my husband, I would've killed him and his so-and-so bitch."

I asked, "Ladan, do you love your husband?"

Her look was questioning. I said, "It's simple. 'Either yes, or no."

She said, "Yes, I love him very much. He is perfect, a great lover, and a very kind father to our child. I adore him, but have never told him this."

For a second a jealous feeling distracted me. Loving feelings hadn't been part of my life for so many years. I began to cry at the realization of how much I had missed and what I had lost. I cried for the loveless, frozen state of my heart, and I cried for the isolation and loneliness. I cried for my entrapment in private and social prisons.

Ladan came close, opening her arms to hold me while I sobbed. Her words had brought a flood of suppressed emotions. Memories of my late teens flashed before me. I had been one of the luckiest and happiest girls in town.

In times of emotional pain and desperation, I would run to Bernard in my imagination, where his love would comfort me. But he had left and forgotten about me in less than a year. There was no man to whom I could turn.

Poor Ladan assumed I was crying because of my husband's betrayal and tried to comfort me, not realizing God was answering my prayer. Still holding me and caressing my hair, she said, "Don't worry Linda. Please stop crying. Everything will work out."

I softly pulled away and looked into her eyes, saying "Ladan, I prayed for this day."

Her jaw dropped, trying to make sense of what I had said.

"What do you mean you prayed for this?" she asked. "Who would want this? You were just crying your eyes out. I don't understand."

I tried to explain. "Ladan, if you know what my life is like, why are you surprised? I am tired. I want to change my life, to leave Bijan and this country. I don't belong in this marriage or Iran.

"I am not safe or happy at home or outside. Remember how that woman cursed us? I can't tiptoe around anymore or subject my son to the mental torture, either."

I continued, "I am going to share something very secret and personal." I told her about the passport form and the incredible danger involved, but that I was ready to risk it. I would rather walk across the minefield I now faced than remain in the status quo. I would be free from Bijan, die in prison, or stay and die more each day.

At the elevator while leaving, Ladan implored me to change my mind. "This is impossible. I know your life is terrible. The situation is heart-wrenching. But prison really will be worse.

"I don't think you understand what goes on in Evin Prison. They will regularly rape and brutalize you. Aren't you afraid of that? Beatings, torture, and starvation. They will destroy you, Linda."

"Ladan, I am already being beaten, tortured and raped by my husband. Have you ever been beaten by your husband because you didn't want to have sex with him? I have to take that risk or surrender forever. I will not surrender," I replied.

With gallows humor, she added, "Don't tell me when you leave for your appointment. The wait for you to return will kill me."

I put my hand on her shoulder as comfort and promised not to tell. Gently, I pressed her toward the open door. "You are going to do it! You just confirmed it..." Her voice trailed off as the door closed.

Lying on the couch, looking out the windows at the blue sky and patches of clouds, I saw the sunshine and the carefree birds singing from their perch on a wire. What at first looked like a bird approaching turned out to be a plane.

Despite being alone, I called out, "God, will the day come when my son and I can fly away?"

Soon I drifted off to sleep, hoping for sweet dreams.

Thirty-Four

I awoke just in time to pick up James at school. It was only a few blocks away, a pleasant walk down Pahlavi Street.

My sister-in-law once told me that Bijan had confessed to her that even watching me walk in front of him, makes him love me even more. What happened? Maybe I don't walk the same way anymore.

I arrived at school a few minutes early and had to wait on the street side of the school entry gate.

"*Salam, Khanom,*" I heard someone say.

It was Farsi for "Hello, Lady."

I looked at the bold stranger with raised eyebrows. He politely introduced himself, waiting for me to respond. Ignoring social norms, I kept quiet.

He said, "I noticed you long ago, coming to pick up your son. You are always alone, never accompanied by your husband, so I thought..."

I didn't let him finish. He chose the wrong day to flirt. I knew where this was going.

I asked, "When you pick up your child, do you bring the dynasty?"

He took a step back, unamused.

"Wow, someone woke up on the wrong side of the bed today," he said.

I snapped back, "Not the wrong side of the bed, you chose the wrong person to talk to."

I stepped away from him as the gate opened and children came running to their parents. My son rushed to me, and I went to give him a hug. When I kissed him, he pulled back saying, "Mama, I am not a little boy anymore, don't kiss me in front of my friends."

This was new. He was growing up.

Then the man from earlier approached.

"Can I give you a ride?" he asked.

What was wrong with him? I politely declined, "No, thank you, we want to walk." I thought to myself, "Men are like ships without anchors, aimlessly floating from harbor to harbor."

At dinner that evening, James seemed worried. He told me that his teacher said listening to music was forbidden because it is a sin in Islam.

"He asked us to let him know if our parents listen to music at home," he said. "What I should do? I love music, and you always listen to it."

The regime was turning our kids into spies, loyal eyes and ears to spread their control over people's lives. I couldn't imagine life without music. It has always been medicine for my soul.

What God or true holy man ever said music was evil? I wasn't going to stop playing music in my home. Should I teach my child to lie?

But I had to say, "Honey, we listen to music in our home. The only thing you need to remember is don't tell them. That's all. IF they ask, just say no. Do you think you can do that? Just say no."

He seemed relieved, replying, "Yes, one word is good, 'No.'"

The regime wanted to dictate how we lived in our home sanctuaries. They had trapped our children between two very different cultures and beliefs. They planned to brainwash them since it was too late to try to change the parents.

Later that evening after homework, James and I watched a music video. He loved the Bee Gee's and knew all their names. We danced around the apartment to "Staying Alive."

He was so happy. That is all I wanted for him. After our disco party, he took his bath, put on his pajamas, and came to me for a good-night kiss.

"Don't forget to pray, Sweetheart," I said. "Ask God for blessings of freedom."

He had a puzzled look, asking, "What's freedom?"

Now I had the puzzled face. I was not sure I could explain freedom to a seven-year-old.

"Well, let's say you enjoy listening to music," I said. "You listen to it whenever you want to, knowing that it is not harming anyone nor is it forbidden by God. That is freedom. You are free to listen to music, without the fear of being caught by someone who doesn't like it.

"When others believe they have a right to make that decision for you, they have denied you your freedom."

I was surprised when he said, "I am going to pray for freedom. Good night, Mama! I love you, and I love freedom."

What a day. There was no sign of Bijan. But for the first time in a long while, I was anxious for him to return, not out of love, but because I was awaiting his reaction to the receipt taped to the mirror.

My restless soul had me pacing from room to room. Though my mind was unable to function, my heart was in pain. I needed a break from what life had become.

I opened the window and turned on the Bee Gees. Sitting on the floor with my back against the couch, I waited. Robin Gibb's sweet and sad voice filled the room with his song "I Started a Joke." Like in the lyrics, it seemed the joke was on me.

Two hours passed before I heard the key in the door, just after midnight. In stepped Bijan, drunk. He was surprised to find the lights on and me still up. He tried to stand still but wobbled as he waited for me to say something.

I wondered how he could have driven. We looked at each other in silence. I stopped the music and turned on the TV. Finally, he asked why I was up.

"It's late, let's go to bed," he said.

"No," I replied, "You go ahead, I can't sleep." Bijan went to the bedroom.

Almost immediately, he returned with the receipt in his hand. Pointing at it, he asked, "What is this?"

What a shameless bastard to question me. Was he playing games with me or was he acting? "How low can you go Bijan?"

"Aren't you man enough to admit you 'took' another wife?

"That is the receipt of the ring you bought for her, whoever she is, but that is not my point. The point is that you are a low life. I'm ashamed to be your wife."

I said what I felt, choosing fight over flight, though this approach had not served me well in the past. Bijan took one step toward me as I was still sitting on the floor, and kicked his other foot directly into my face. He jumped back in shock when he saw the damage and rushed for the phone.

It was over as fast as it had started. I couldn't see from my right eye, and the pain was overwhelming. I held in my screams to keep from waking my son, but my moaning, I could not control. I was tired of screaming. I had enough of muffling my screams because my husband had hurt me.

Pulling myself up by the arm of the couch, I used the furniture as support to make my way to the bathroom. The face I had taken for granted all my life was now unrecognizable. Massive swelling on the right side had engulfed my eye. What if he had been blind me?

That moment was the closest I came to killing Bijan. But motherhood prevented me.

Crying uncontrollably, I wanted to call my father and ask him to take me to the hospital, but I feared what he would do to Bijan or worse, I feared he would have a heart attack.

Someone must have arrived because I could hear muffled voices through the bathroom door. Then came a knock. I froze in my agony.

The knocking continued. Then my brother-in-law spoke.

"Linda, it's me," Behnam said. "I am here to take you to the emergency room. May I come in please?"

As usual, Bijan had called his brother to clean up another mess.

I asked him to wait for me to get ready.

I finally opened the door. When my brother-in-law saw me, his jaw dropped.

"Oh, dear God," he gasped, covering his mouth.

His reaction seemed to confirm that he, too, thought he'd blinded me. What a victory that would have been for Bijan. In the end, there wouldn't be anything left of me to escape this house.

Bijan was nowhere to be seen as we left.

The trip was silent, dark and frightening. I'd rather die than lose an eye. I could only pray: "Father in Heaven, please see what is happening to me. Why won't you rescue me? God, I need my eye, let it be okay. I need it to survive. Please help me escape this country. Please bless me, Lord."

Patients packed the waiting area, all of them were staring at me like I had come from another planet, but I couldn't hide my face.

The doctor said he couldn't do much. Until the swelling went down, there was no way to know the extent of damage to the eye. He prescribed something and referred me to an eye specialist for a final diagnosis. Thank God he did not ask how it happened. What would I say?

Back home, I asked Behnam to stay until morning and take James to school. I didn't want him to see me this way, but how long could I hide?

Standing in the middle of my bedroom, I looked around the cold, empty room. When I stepped onto the balcony in the early morning darkness, a cold breeze sent a chill straight to my bones. I sat there for a cigarette, staring at the faint light of the horizon.

Suddenly, my passport appointment came to mind. I couldn't remember the date and went to check it. I was relieved that I had a month for my face to heal before the appointment. I was hopeful that I would heal and be more presentable by then. But what if I was blind? The only choice would be to move back to my parent's house, divorce or not.

Thirty-Five

I awoke on the balcony to the cacophony of life in the city. Rushing to check my still-throbbing face, what I saw was a shock. It had gotten worse. The cuts on the right side of my face looked like a raw steak. I tried applying antibiotic cream, but it stung too badly.

My face bore the worst physical damage I had ever sustained as a result of Bijan's violence. I wondered what had gone so wrong. In the beginning, he acted like nothing was too good for me. He hated being apart from me, even for a day. He gave me vacations, took me shopping, and even found whatever food I might be craving, no matter how inconvenient. My wish was his command. Now his command would be my death.

I thought back to an earlier trip to the Caspian Sea. We had stopped for lunch and bought an assortment of seafood. I had asked for rice, but the waiter said they were out of rice. Bijan stood up and said he'd be back soon, before disappearing into the back of the restaurant.

As we kept talking and busily ate our food, the waiter returned with a big plate of steaming rice. Grinning, he said, "I brought this dish from my kitchen. It was well worth the trip. I got paid handsomely." Bijan had made this happen for me.

But the things that endeared me to him were short lived. How could one person change so drastically? I had not changed; I had remained faithful; why couldn't he?

At times of pain and despair, I wished to cheat on him, but I had promised myself not to pleasure another to get revenge on Bijan. The same man, who would have picked the stars from the sky one by one for me if I had wished for them, hit me during my eighth month of pregnancy and now may have blinded me.

No one had ever raised a hand to me. How much was I supposed to sacrifice as a woman or as a mother? How could I have ended up a punching bag for the husband who, supposedly, was to love and care for me?

I couldn't even cry. The tears had run dry. I was angry at myself for allowing this. On top of everything, women, wives, and mothers had no rights in Islamic Iran. I had no hope for social justice!

Taking another look at my eye, a wave of anger weighed on me so heavily that I collapsed on the floor, screaming like a wounded animal. Inside, something was breaking. It had shattered me. The fear and frustration of life under Bijan and the Regime had destroyed me. My immense hatred demanded an outlet. I wanted to destroy what was destroying me.

I fantasized about beating Bijan like he had done to me for all these years. I imagined torturing and killing the leaders and guards of the revolution, the way they had stolen people's lives throughout Iran. I would have no mercy on any of them if I had the chance.

Regaining my composure, I rose to face the day with even more determination to escape. An eerie silence filled the house. James was at school. He had been gone for the weekend thanks to Behnam who, after school, had taken him to my in-laws so that I could have some time to heal and spare my child the trauma of seeing me looking like a monster.

If I had ever come home to my mom looking the way I did, I would have had nightmares, I am sure. James had been through enough, just having Bijan as his father.

Two days were not enough. I had asked my mother in law to tell James that I had fallen and hurt my eye or anything to prepare him mentally. Behnam was going to stay with us for few days. It was a relief to have help, but I also resented that Bijan was off the hook with his family always rescuing him.

When the bell rang, I opened the gate, and the door to the apartment then ran to find something to cover my eye. Then I heard James call, "Mama, Mama where are you? I'm home."

He ran into my bedroom before I could answer. The big grin on his face disappeared when he saw me. Frozen in his tracks, he had a look of sheer horror. He screamed louder than I thought possible for a boy his size. Then, he ran out. My son was afraid of me.

I heard him crying, as his uncle tried to comfort him. I felt horrible. At that moment, I hated Bijan more than a human being is capable of hating someone. Hate had poisoned every fiber of my being. James was too innocent to be subjected to this horror.

It would be another week before the swelling, and my son's shock subsided. My eye still would not open properly. A specialist was to look at it that day. I almost didn't want to know the result. The thought of losing my eyesight was devastating. My life would be subject to yet another torment. Tired of the incessant battles, I got ready as slowly as possible.

My brother-in-law and I were on our way out when the phone rang. "Hello," I answered. After a brief pause, Bijan called my name, "Linda, hi, Baby, I know you are going to the doctor. I wish I could take you there, My Love, I am so sorry, I..."

I had to stop him. Hearing his voice was like another attack. This time, I returned the attack, "You sick animal. Just stay away from me. The only thing you can do for me is give me a divorce. Other than that, we have nothing to talk about."

Standing at my doctor's office with my heart pounding, knees shaking, and breathing labored, I couldn't move to open the door. Behnam's hand on my shoulder gently nudged me forward. His face expressed his understanding.

Luckily, I was sent straight to the examining room. A heavy set, middle aged nurse, with large buttocks and an even bigger chest, stepped into the room, throwing a cold smile in my direction.

"I am Nurse Aghate, the doctor's assistant," she said, "I'll wash your eye before the exam."

A medical station made up of all sorts of equipment filled the center of the room. Suspended next to a dark leather chair, was a neatly organized tray of smaller tools. As Nurse Aghate cleaned my eye, an adjacent door opened and a handsomely dressed elderly doctor stepped in.

With a bright smile, he pointed me toward the chair. The doctor rolled his chair toward me, taking a few small instruments from the tray. He carefully began to maneuver under my eyelid. The painful process included using different lights that I followed with my wounded eye.

After more painful tests, he finally spoke. "The emergency doctor said that he was fairly certain you had lost your eyesight. He mentioned how horrible you looked, using the analogy of, "Joe Frazier after a match with Mohammed Ali."

He continued, "I believe in karma. Try to remember where and when you did a good deed because today is your reward. Your eyesight is fine. You are one lucky lady. I am very happy for you.

"I will prescribe medication, and I want to see you in a week's time. One more thing, never forget what I am about to say. Don't let anyone, for any reason, do this to you ever again. Do you hear me?"

I couldn't say a word as tears rolled down my face. I gave him the biggest hug I could give. He was taken aback, given I was not even allowed to shake his hand under Islamic law.

I was laughing and crying at the same time; I was beyond happy. God had spared my eyesight. He had also saved my life for all those years. I wondered, "What was His plan, why was he keeping me here?"

The day before had been my bleakest; today was one of my happiest. The thought of returning to the scene of the crime sent a cold shiver through me.

Thirty-Six

Bijan had not been home since the night he kicked me in the face. I was relieved. I preferred he stay away, for good. But entering the house, we saw Bijan and my in-laws seated in the living room. I nodded a greeting to my in-laws, then turned to Bijan.

"What the hell are you doing here?" I said angrily, taking advantage of the presence of witnesses. "You can't come back here until we get a divorce and I have moved out. My stomach turns when I look at your face.

"You make me sick, you psycho animal. I am done with you, Bijan. I've been done with you since a few weeks into our marriage, the first time I asked you for a divorce. Remember?"

Bijan stood and listened. But had his parents not been there, he likely already would have attacked. He finally spoke, "Linda, I will do whatever you want me to. If you want me to go, I will go.

"But just give me ten minutes to explain few things. That's why I've asked my family to be here, so you all can hear me out. Only ten minutes, please, then I promise I will go."

It was impossible to tolerate him. Everyone was staring, waiting for me to speak. Knowing I had to get his signature on the divorce as well as on a visa and passport if I succeeded in getting one, I decided to lay out my case and force his hand in providing what I needed. There was no time for him to talk.

"For almost ten years I have suffered in this loveless, meaningless, merciless, and barbaric life," I said. "It is as if you stole my best years. If I stay with you and can survive your attacks for the next ten, then twenty years will have been wasted.

"I don't understand you, Bijan. How could you want to live with me when you know I don't love you. I'd rather die than be touched by you. You know damn well James is the reason you have kept me in this prison. Don't you feel any shame at keeping someone by force and terror?

"'Look at me Bijan. Look at my eye and face. This is the consequence of life with you, pain and nothing else. I am saying this in front of your family because I am serious, and you need to hear me.

"I plan to risk my life for a passport. If I succeed, I want your signature so I can leave the country. I want you to arrange a visa for me. And I want you to leave now. I can't stand you."

As if none of them expected these words, they sat quietly with surprised expressions. Addressing my mother-in-law I said, "If your daughter was standing here brutally beaten and almost blinded at the hands of your son-in-law, would you still sit there, surprised?"

She didn't look at me but meekly replied, "No." For a moment, I felt sorry for her. She probably had no authority to express anything, her entire life.

I told Bijan to take James for couple of days, that I needed time alone to pull myself together. He went to the bedroom, packed, and returned to the living room, looking at me like a beaten dog, asking if I needed anything. I answered, "Did you pack for your son as well?"

He seemed absent, but turned and went to James' room, returning with a backpack a few minutes later.

He asked again if I needed anything. I didn't bother to look at him. I said, "Whatever I need, you don't have." Bijan didn't reply, took his bag, and they all left.

If by some miracle I were to get my passport, I planned to travel to the farthest place on the planet. It didn't matter where, just far from here.

Within a few days, I had received another letter from the authorities, informing me that a large demand for passports meant an appointment delay of a month-and-a-half.

The letter had extinguished the last flicker of light in my dark world. The despair, anger, pain, humiliation, and bitterness were winning the war for my soul. The wait might cost me my life.

My heart broke. How was I going to survive forty-five days living with Bijan or avoiding trouble with Islamic guards with their constant presence outside? Even a simple shopping trip could end in arrest. I had always been an independent person. Despite the harsh consequences, it was near impossible for me to shut up and obey Bijan or the Regime.

After a week, Bijan was back at home, acting as if nothing had happened, gushing of his love and feigning the acts of a great husband. History showed this phony persona to be the precursor for his next attack.

My constant sense of trauma was like a hair trigger, waiting to enrage him without thought of the consequences. But I decided to keep the peace this time. I needed him to permit my exit from the country until I reached the safety of freedom, then I could apply for divorce.

It became a challenge to avoid him by pretending to be busy in the kitchen or spending time in James' room, either helping him with homework or reading books together.

But nighttime was a different story. To avoid being touched by him, I forced myself to stay at the sink washing clean dishes until late at night to be sure he was asleep before I went to bed. I didn't want him to touch me.

In the darkness of our bedroom, my responsibility as a wife became the most unbearable part of my life. Being in bed with him made me feel like a cheap whore, letting him take my body without affection or feeling.

As Bijan moaned with pleasure, I cried bitterly in silence. He never noticed. During those times, I would wish him death, despite my religion's teaching that it was a one-way ticket to hell. It seemed worth it.

I had missed out on a happy life and true love. I had hoped for a warm home, where there was dancing, singing, chatting, going out with friends, watching a movie with family, laughing at silly jokes. These were mine, once, but now they felt light years away. One day, I would have them again.

Thirty-Seven

At last, the day that could change my life was near. Tomorrow would be my passport appointment and, I'd hoped, a new destiny, not one that ended with me in prison. I had decided that, if caught, I would commit suicide. Death was preferable to torture and rape.

I knew that would not be fair to James; I was his mother, sister, brother, and pal. Who else would do what I do for him? Who would love him?

But risking my life for our freedom by attempting to get a passport was our only chance to escape the country. Either way, I would die eventually, because I was certain Bijan would surely kill me.

I went to see my family, as it might be the last time if anything went wrong the next day. I soaked everything in, mentally recording their voices in my heart, looking deeply into their faces.

I wanted it etched into my mind...the paintings and the pictures on the walls, the design and color of the curtains, the furniture, Dad's favorite chair, Mom's special coffee cup. Everything in the house had even more meaning now.

Hiding my emotional rollercoaster ride was becoming impossible. I had the urge to hug each one of them every few minutes but feared making them suspicious. I would not worry them this day.

And only God knew what tomorrow would bring. Seeing them, all of us talking and laughing as a family, began to weaken my resolve. Even getting the passport likely meant never seeing them again.

I found an excuse to go to my old room, where I had been happiest. Looking out on the familiar street, the shops and shopkeepers, whom I knew well, the passersby, the trees, everything seemed as it used to be - everything but my life.

Walking to the center of the room, I visualized ten years before, when I was still a happy, carefree teen. So many memories returned including time spent sharing secrets with Narine, playing music, dancing, and having friends over.

I could still see Bernard sitting on my bed, singing and playing his guitar. I remembered birthdays and Christmases we celebrated here. I bitterly recalled the day when Bijan was in this room, waiting for me to pack and leave with him. Then it occurred to me that reminiscing in my room was keeping me in the past. My attention needed to be in the present.

I never knew acting could be this difficult; I used to act with no problem. But the movie scripts were not my story, to be played by me. The dreaded moment of leaving approached. Although crying inside, I managed to look casual and tried to smile.

Outside, I was free to have the cry of my life. I knew I was risking my family's lives, as well. The Regime might not distinguish my actions from theirs. If I were to get arrested, it would kill my father, and my mother would die soon after. My siblings would become orphans.

Later that day, after dinner, Bijan watched TV in the living room, while I spent time with James in his room. He loved his room. Above his bed was a huge poster of Pinocchio dancing as Geppetto played the accordion. On the other side, scattered toys, fire trucks, racing cars, roller skates, and storybooks covered the floor.

Next to the window in the corner was his desk; above it on the wall was his favorite picture of himself, from when he was two years old. I don't know why he liked that one so much.

I tucked him in, read a book, and wished him angel dreams before kissing him good night, on what might be our last one together. All that I might be giving up brought me to my knees next to his bed. I felt as if I was on the verge of a breakdown. Was he going to grow up without me?

I held his hand until he fell asleep and stayed to watch his innocent face. It was my duty to give my child a safe and loving environment, so he could grow up happy and fulfilled. I would never accomplish that living with his father and the Islamic regime.

For hours, I stayed with him, smelling him, caressing his hair, just looking at him. I couldn't get enough. Eventually, I turned off the light, wiped my tears, and stepped out of the room.

Still watching TV, Bijan asked me to sit and talk. I was numb. Today, I had already bid farewell to those I loved most in life. It felt as if my ability to produce emotions was gone. In a fog, my brain could not make out what Bijan was saying. His words disappeared into thin air before reaching my ears.

I tried to concentrate, sat more rigid, looked straight at his mouth as he formed the sounds. Nothing. He turned the television off and reached for my hands, holding them gently, as he said, in a worried tone, "Linda, what's wrong with you? Is it fear of the unknown you will face tomorrow?"

This, I heard. I said, "I'm fine. Yes, it's the thought of to-morrow."

Standing, I moved my hands away and walked toward the bedroom. He followed, got undressed, and laid on the bed. I only hoped for a deep, dreamless sleep, like a coma.

I got undressed and into bed, turning on the lamp to read a while. I was avoiding Bijan's touch. I was preoccupied with the significance of this night.

For the first time in my life, I had no idea where I would be the next day at this time. I went to look at my son one more time and kissed his forehead before returning to say my prayers. Bijan was snoring like a locomotive.

Up early, it was a long and leisurely breakfast, as if to postpone the inevitable. The three of us headed for the passport office.

Through the car window, I witnessed the further transfor-mation of Tehran. Once upon a time, it was full of happy people with smiling faces, shining eyes, filled with the joy of life. There was laughter of children playing and beautifully dressed people strolling through the bustling streets.

All that had vanished. Now, all anyone could see was misery. Drab shades of black, dark blue, dark brown, or gray covered everything but frowns and eyes which were flashing rage and despair. People could not move about as freely, so many stayed indoors.

"Linda, we're here," Bijan said, as he pulled to the curb a block away from my appointment, a safe distance, should my plan go awry. They would wait in the car for me - assuming I would return.

Stepping out of the car, I waved goodbye and obsessively checked my clothing as I walked. My hair had to be perfectly covered by the scarf, with not a strand exposed. My dress, buttoned up to my neck and with long sleeves, covered me to the middle of my feet.

Soon I was standing in front of the building, in front of a huge metal door. Across the threshold was a large yard-like area. A guard pointed toward a staircase leading to the next floor, where another guard would direct me further. I thanked him, took few steps toward the stairs, but stopped before the first step.

This was my last chance to turn back. I quickly went over the pros and cons in my mind. If I take the stairs, there would be no turning back. If I just turn around and go home, I would surely die at Bijan's hands one day.

I began the climb, feeling as ready as I could be for what was ahead. In the middle of a huge area with several desks and filing cabinets, stood a tall man in an army uniform, holding himself as if he was a high-ranking officer. His jacket bore star pins, but I had no idea of their significance.

I panicked, but he had already noticed me, probably thinking I needed directions. Approaching, he politely asked, "You look lost. Is there a specific department you are looking for?"

I read his bronze nametag. His last name had the word "Shah" in it. I thanked him for his kindness and said I was looking for the passport office. Then, stupidly, I thought, I randomly commented, "I see from your nametag that you are one of us."

Immediately I sensed I may have dug my grave. This was no time for careless self-sabotage.

To my relief and surprise, he smiled as if he liked what I had said. Then, after making sure no one was in hearing distance, he asked, "Are you leaving the country?"

I replied, "Yes, I want to leave before I die, the sooner, the better. It's easy to be a foreigner, in a foreign country, but to feel as if you are a foreigner in your country is tragic. Maybe you should leave too, Sir."

Without answering, he called a guard over and ordered him to direct me to the passport receiving room. "Make sure she gets her passport," he said, "then report back to your post."

The guard saluted and asked me to follow. I thanked my army "angel." The guard took me through winding corridors while fear crept over me, once again. My application contained my real name, but the receipt I had brought was filled out using a man's name. I expected them to ask for the receipt before releasing my passport.

There was nothing I could do now. After what seemed like endless hallways, we arrived at a room that was divided by a glass partition. One side was for those wanting a passport, the other held rows of cubbyholes containing thousands of the coveted passports.

Here I was, near the end of my mission. In a few moments, either my passport would be in my hands, or I would be in handcuffs. I felt faint.

A guard politely asked for my receipt from beyond the glass wall. This was it. The moment I dreaded. Without faltering, I looked straight at him and slowly said, "You see, that's the problem. As I mentioned earlier, I couldn't find my receipt, but I have my picture ID with me, the proof that it is me. My name is Linda..."

He quietly interrupted me saying, "I know who you are, Ma'am. Please wait a second." He disappeared for few moments, and then emerged holding a passport. I couldn't believe it.

I was expecting to be surrounded by revolutionary guards. Instead, the guard came closer, handed me the passport, and with a sheepish grin asked, "Could I have your autograph, please?"

I gave him a big smile as I buried the passport in my purse. I was never happier to give an autograph. I contained myself as I slowly walked away. I wanted to run at top speed. On my way back, I noticed my Army Angel had gone back to heaven. His mission had also been accomplished.

At the staircase, I descended two steps at a time. It was just 15 more steps to the big metal entrance. Then, I was out of the building and free to run as fast as I could. I thought they could be following me. I sprinted without stopping until I reached the car.

The insights I gained that day gave me an entirely new outlook on what is possible in life. Moving in the direction of our desires with faith and perseverance despite the obstacles no matter how circumstances appear is how we are meant to live.

The fear and worry had been unnecessary. Thank God I didn't let my mental state stop me. I also believed that divine intervention took charge to save my life. I am in awe at how things worked out on that life changing day. Never had I planned to give an autograph or be comforted by a "Shah."

In the political climate of the day, something that should have been simple, like getting a passport, had become a huge challenge. I had overcome that challenge and had my ticket to freedom. Next, I had to navigate whatever danger remained between that day and my final escape with my son.

Thirty-Eight

Being out in public was entirely unpleasant. I never left the house without going through my "safety" checklist. I was not going to end up in any arguments with Khomeini's men.

Long scarf, tightly tied, check.

No hair is visible, check.

Long and loose pants, covering my legs, check.

Long sleeves, covering my arms, check.

Maxi coat/dress, buttoned to my chin, check.

No makeup or nail polish, check.

Expressionless, like a zombie, check.

The streets were without music. I couldn't even hear birds singing anymore.

I began to visit my family as often as possible; knowing that soon I would be gone and most likely would never be back. I also started to pray more, thanking God and asking for his continued mercy for my child and me.

There were times when I could see how James adored his father. He needed his dad, despite Bijan rarely being home, again. My son was always happy when he was spending time with his father. Though I believed a child needs both parents to make a loving and safe home, Bijan and I had failed to do that for James.

If I could have trusted Bijan to be a dedicated father, I might have considered leaving the boy in his care. But knowing my husband, I couldn't bring myself to do it.

The thought of Bijan neglecting James tortured me. But if I take him, he may forever blame me for divorcing his father and putting distance between them. At some point, soon, I would have to make this decision.

Meanwhile, it was 1984 and the war with Iraq raged on. Images of war and casualties from both sides filled the newspapers. We heard that Iran was blocking Iraqi oil exports through the Persian Gulf. Perhaps this would make it harder for Saddam to finance his army.

Life remained fragile. Any day something major could go wrong. The country, not long ago an island of stability in the Middle East, had become a place of darkness and fear. For most people, life had become a struggle to survive. There was no time to think about life's true meaning and purpose.

While working to obtain a visa, I faced yet another problem. No embassy was giving visas to Iranians. It seemed no country wanted us.

This left one option, contact a smuggler and leave via the mountain, valley, and river, ending up either in Pakistan, Turkey, or Afghanistan, and from there, God only knew. No, this was not the solution for my son.

After asking Bijan to investigate the possibilities, he came back just a few days later, saying he could arrange a visa. I couldn't remember being this happy with him, and asked "How is that possible?"

Smiling, he replied, "With the power of money, Sweetheart."

I did not understand what he meant. He explained that he had met a man who said he could get visas from two different European embassies.

"The choice is yours, Babe, where ever you want to go. But remember, they are for sale. It is going to cost us, dearly."

It figured...the only way to get a visa was to do it the unethical way. Such was the state of the country. I expected as much, but if that's what it would take, that's what I would do, regardless of the cost.

We agreed that at the end of the school year, during summer break, James and I would leave Iran. After a few months, Bijan would leave, too, but he would have to rely on smugglers. I had no intention of reuniting with him, whatever his plans.

In just a few weeks, I got my passport with a stamped entry visa to a European country. Hail to the power of money!

Only a few months remained. I continued to be extra careful outside the house and to placate Bijan as needed to avoid any confrontation.

It was not going to be easy to live through, especially being so close to freedom. My new future was within my reach, and I was anxious to live it. I had to, no...I would survive.

The country I chose to go to after leaving Iran was non-English-speaking. Their language was foreign to me. Without knowing a single person, having no relatives or friends, I wondered what I was doing.

How would James learn or study? How would we communicate with others? What kind of work could I possibly find? Thinking about the unknown was frightening, but if I could survive the present, I would survive the future.

Days were passing very slowly, and those days turned into weeks. One evening, Bijan called to say he was on his way with a surprise.

I wondered what it could be. Divorce papers? A new mistress? Another wife?

It was strange to feel so calm about any of those options. But the fact was, there was no hurt, humiliation, or jealousy. The reason? I didn't love him. He had lost that privilege long ago. My total concentration was on my future.

He arrived home as I was setting the dinner table. Throwing his keys down, he took an envelope out of his pocket, saying, "This is the surprise I told you about."

I opened it to find two plane tickets and noticed the date of departure was three weeks away.

I thanked him, and said, "Now we have to get some foreign currency for my trip."

Bijan looked disappointed, saying, "I was expecting to see you jump for joy, rush into my arms, and kiss me."

"Don't get me wrong," I said. "I'm grateful to have the tickets, but when was the last time I jumped into your arms and kissed you? I don't remember, do you?"

He had hurt me so much that none of these gestures would compensate. He didn't answer, and the conversation ended.

A few days later, Bijan came home with enough foreign currency to cover my trip and living expenses for at least a year. Our money, like our lives, had lost value since the revolution.

Bijan was anxious about how I could get the cash out of the country without being caught. We'd heard many stories about fundamentalist guards controlling security at the airports and would do body searches if they were suspicious or just for their perverted pleasure.

224 | STELLA RILEY

Passengers were accompanied by their families so that they could return valuable items to their homes. Little did the regime know that the most valuable thing leaving the country was its people.

After brainstorming a safe place to hide the money, we ended up unscrewing the metal from the edges of my suitcase, rolling the notes and hiding them all around the inside of the tubing. I hoped that no one else had been caught using the same seemingly ingenious idea.

Each night, Bijan would pace around the suitcase, saying, "This won't work. They'll find it. It's dangerous."

I would escort him out of the room, saying, "Just forget about the money. It will work out. I know it's dangerous, but isn't danger our constant companion in this country?"

My flight was in two days. Just forty-eight more hours before I would embrace my dream, change my life, live with free will, and most of all, be happy again. How many years had I waited? Underlying my joy was sadness for leaving my family behind, especially with the country at war.

Saddam Hussein thought he could just come in to, conquer and change our borders, adding the southern part of Iran where the oil fields were to his country and leave with Khomeini defeated.

During the Shah's regime, he would have never dared to even dream about attacking Iran. But years later, he found the Iranians still fighting, regardless of the ruling mullahs.

Thirty-Nine

My trip didn't need much preparation. I packed to give the impression of a short vacation. I left behind my winter clothes, important documents, books, and even pictures. One suitcase was full of my son's clothes and toys and one with my things.

Though I was thrilled to be escaping, there coexisted a sense of misery and depression with the awareness that I was living the final hours of my life as I had known it, where all my memories were made, good or bad.

I was pulling up my roots to float weightlessly on the winds of life. But, of course, I always returned to the certainty that anything was better than marital and social slavery.

Home alone, I looked around the house, remembering every single violent incident and the days and weeks of suffering in silence. There were few happy recollections. Out of 10 years, three-thousand-six-hundred-fifty days, maybe 50 were happy.

Here I was, a thirty-one-year-old, unhappy woman trying to heal, stand tall and confront an unknown future in a strange country with responsibility for another person. But if I wanted us both to live free with basic human rights, it would take leaving my family, my roots, and my country.

That night Bijan came home drunk, with a dangerous look in his eyes. Couldn't he control himself for two more days? The too-familiar physical sense of danger swept my body.

He demanded dinner, so I asked him to check the fridge for something quick. That was all it took, my tiptoeing around and attempts to keep him calm had been fruitless.

He grabbed my shoulders forcefully and screamed in my face: "I didn't come home for cold food. What have you been you doing the whole day, visiting your mama?"

Looking straight into his eyes, I replied, "Yes."

He pushed me backward to the floor, jumped on top of me, and began a brutal attack. I defended myself with all my strength. I was not going to die this close to escape. His intoxication made it difficult for him to balance as I rolled forcefully out from under him and stood to run. I had to get out of the house.

I reached the door, with blood streaming from my nose and a broken fingernail. Fearing the neighbors would see me, I fled to the roof, where I hid for the next few hours. My time contemplating life with Bijan reinforced my will to live and to get out of the country. Even if he managed to be smuggled out, he would never see me again.

The most consequential day of my life finally arrived. When Bijan's brothers arrived to take me to the airport, they found Bijan on the couch, holding James. I had not spoken to him since coming back into the apartment late the night before.

I donned my Islamic uniform for the last time and moved to the door. Bijan came over and put his arms around me, wishing me a safe journey of all things. He said he loved me and would miss me until we could reunite. I wondered if he felt my full-body cringe. I wanted to scream at him, but walking out the door was the better revenge.

Half the population seemed to be at the airport escaping the country with me. Anyone who could leave seemed to be leaving the country all at the same time. Posters of Khomeini and his gang of mullahs plastered the walls.

After saying good-bye to Bijan's brothers and wishing them a safe life, I took my son's hand and pulled my luggage toward check-in. A guard approached me in line, demanding to inspect my bags. I suppressed my anger, knowing it was not too late for these thugs to ruin my plans.

I asked, "Which would you prefer I open?"

Luckily, he chose my bag, the one without the frame full of cash. Seeing only clothes and shoes, he left without a word, his sick ego appeased.

An hour and many checkpoints later, I had my boarding pass in hand, which also covered my son. We had one more checkpoint, the body search station. The guards were female, but still the process was dehumanizing. A female guard, who was overly interested in a pearl ring I was wearing, stopped me.

She asked me to remove it, the only ring I wore besides my wedding band. Passing it to her, I was determined not to part with it. She looked at it from all sides and flatly said it I would not be allowed to take it out of the country.

In the middle of explaining to her that I had no family member to give it to, a male guard approached, ordering, "Give her ring back and let her go."

I slid it back where it belonged and headed to the plane.

James took the window seat, and I sat next to him, handing him a book to read to keep his mind off leaving his dad. The plane taxied and soon we were in the air.

Thinking about the challenges ahead and seeing Tehran's apartment buildings below, I remembered having stood on the terrace, watching planes go by and praying that one day we would be on one of them. I couldn't help but to think of the countless women at that very moment, with broken bodies, hearts, and pride, who also were standing on their balconies wishing to be on a plane.

That is when I stood to pull the scarf off my head, rejecting all things Islamic. But the stewardess quickly advised that I wait a few minutes until the plane crossed the Iranian border, "then it would be safe."

"I've waited for this moment for so many years," I said, "I think I can wait a few more minutes."

I said a prayer of gratitude to God for Him having put us on this plane. Facing an unknown future, I would need his blessings now more than ever. He was all we had. Thanks to Him, I had staged my revolution.

It would lead me to a new life, without undue fear, pain, and torment. My simple wish was to live a life not dictated by anyone. I wanted to live a life based on my abilities, living freely the life I would create for myself.

Little did I know how fulfilling that life would be.

The Beginning . . .